BOOKS BY DAN

BEECHWOOD HARBOR MAGIC MYSTERIES

Murder's a Witch

Twice the Witch

Witch Slapped

Witch Way Home

Along Came a Ghost

Lucky Witch (Fall 2017)

BEECHWOOR HARBOR GHOST MYSTERIES

The Ghost Hunter Next Door

Ghosts Gone Wild

When Good Ghosts Get the Blues (Fall 2017)

INTRODUCTION

There's never a good time for a ghost crisis.

However, it's particularly inconvenient while I'm trying to tackle my first wedding season. Between twelve hour days, an assistant with a case of butter fingers (not the chocolate kind), and the flood of tourists in town, I'm struggling to keep a grip on my sanity.

All I want is three months of peace from the spirit world.

But when local ghosts start going missing, I have to do something.

After all, it's not like they go to the Hamptons.

Missing ghosts, a posthumously alimony-hungry divorcee, and a raging bridezilla. Yup, my bingo card was officially full. Can I get a prize and go home now?

CHAPTER 1

It's a new dawn. A new day. A new life. A new ... everything, and it's stressing me out.

With wedding season in full swing, business at my flower shop was booming. As a rookie florist, the prospect of having to fulfill the small town's floral needs single-handedly was daunting. To say the least. I'd hired an assistant to take some of the pressure off my shoulders, but ... well, let's just say it wasn't working out quite the way I'd planned. In just two excruciating weeks, she'd managed to flood the walk-in cooler, break the coffee machine, and total my brand-new delivery van.

Lizzie Hartwell was a sweet, well-meaning girl with an interest in floral design, an easy smile, and—until a week ago—a clean driving record. I was new to being the boss lady and hadn't yet found a gentle way to let her go. At the same time, summer was here, and I was in desperate need of an extra set of hands to help get me through wedding season—regardless of how clumsy they might be.

When the sound of shattering glass caused me to drop the birds of paradise I was placing in a large-scale tropical arrangement, I started to rethink my Ms. Marshmallow stance.

"Sorry!" Lizzie called from the front of the shop.

"Another one bites the dust," Gwen said from her place at the front counter. She was snooping through the computer that pulled local and online orders.

"*You're* the one who recommended her!" I hissed to my ghostly gal-pal.

Gwen shrugged her translucent shoulders. "I swear, I never noticed the butter-finger thing when she worked as a shampoo girl at Lucky Lady."

I sighed. It wasn't her fault. As Beechwood Harbor's gossip queen, she buzzed through my flower shop on a daily basis to see who was sending flowers to whom—and why. Then she carried the scoop back to the Lucky Lady Salon, where the primo gossip percolated. When Lizzie had answered my help-wanted ad in the local newspaper, Gwen signed off without hesitation.

Still, I couldn't blame her for missing the shy girl's utter lack of hand-eye coordination when there was so much hot gossip zinging around. No, at the end of the day, hiring Lizzie had been my call and I'd have to live with it, at least until I could woman up and let her go. Or until she burned the shop down and I no longer needed an assistant.

I closed my eyes and rubbed my forehead. "Is it really too much to ask that we go one day without something ending up broken?"

"I don't think so," Gwen said, drifting away from the computer.

She doesn't know the meaning of *rhetorical*.

Doing my best to keep the irritation out of my voice, I called, "Everything okay out there?"

"Yeah! I'll get it all cleaned up right away!" came the frantic reply.

I drew in a slow, cleansing breath. "When I hired an assistant, I didn't realize I needed to have padding installed on the floors. I also didn't think that she'd be *assisting* me by putting my van in the body shop for a week," I whispered to Gwen.

Gwen offered a sympathetic frown. "She means well."

I opened my eyes and gave a slight nod. "I know. That's what makes it so hard to get rid of her."

"Not to mention you're super swamped right now." Gwen smiled as she tossed her long, sun-bleached hair over her shoulder, sending her feather earrings jangling. "It's *Four Weddings and a Funeral* over here! Literally!"

"Tell me about it," I grumbled, unable to match her level of enthusiasm. Truthfully, it was all a smidgen overwhelming. I'd gone from a wanderlust world traveler to a one-woman show under the microscope of a tight-knit community that seemed to be closing in on me a little bit more each day. In the past two weeks alone, I'd been forced to quick-talk my way out of three separate offers to set me up on a blind date. The locals wanted to get to know their newest resident and it appeared that the more I tried to close the door, the harder they were willing to push.

All of that was more than enough to keep me just inches from the brink of losing my sanity, but then the ghosts got involved and things went from barely manageable to circus-monkeys-loose-in-department-store crazy in two seconds flat.

"You okay, Scarlet?" Gwen asked when I started massaging my temples.

"I'll be fine," I told her. "I'm just feeling a little frazzled today."

A Cheshire grin spread over her delicate face. "That wouldn't have anything to do with the fact that Lucas is coming back into town tonight, would it?"

"No," I said before heaving a sigh. "It has everything to do with the fact that I am van-less for the rest of the afternoon and have three deliveries to make."

"Doesn't Lizzie have a car?"

"She has *half* of a car," I replied, twisting my lips into a sour pout. "It's one of those mini something-or-others that has no cargo space whatsoever."

Lizzie rounded the corner from the front of the shop into the studio space and carefully dumped a dustbin full of shattered glass into the large trashcan by the back door. She shot me a guilty look. "I'm really sorry, Scarlet. You can take it out of my paycheck."

"That's cute that she still thinks she's getting one." Flapjack, the ghost of my childhood Himalayan cat sauntered into view from underneath my workbench. "If I were you, Scar, I'd give her walking papers before she takes out anything else."

Lizzie was not gifted/cursed with the ability to see ghosts and stood wringing her hands as Flapjack handed down his sentence.

I sidestepped the fluffy ghost and placed a hand on Lizzie's shoulder. "It's all right, Lizzie. Accidents happen."

Flapjack made a sneeze-slash-cough sound that clearly communicated he thought I was being a pushover.

I ignored him. "If you can make a note of what was broken, I'll take it out of the inventory database."

Lizzie looked up at me through her thick lashes, her brown eyes glossy with unshed tears. "Are you sure? You're not going to fire me?"

It was all I could do to keep myself from sighing. Instead, I forced a smile that I hoped came across as warm and shook my head. "I'm not going to fire you, but please try to be careful. I know we've been busy since you started, but it's okay to slow down. We'll handle the workload. Okay?"

GHOSTS GONE WILD

Lizzie gave me a timid smile. "Thank you, Scarlet."

The phone rang and Lizzie sprang into action. "I'll get it!"

"At least she's good at that," Flapjack said as Lizzie rushed to answer the phone by the cash register. "Then again, teenage girls usually are. Heaven knows I suffered through your Chatty Cathy phase."

I frowned down at my one-time pet. "No one asked you to stick around and listen in on all of those calls. It's not like you're bound to me. You could have gone anywhere, done anything. You know what I think? I think you *liked* listening to all those giggly conversations, just like you *liked* hanging around for my slumber parties and birthday parties. You even followed me on my first date!"

Gwen covered her mouth to stifle a laugh but her shaking shoulders gave her away. "Aww, Flapjack, I always knew you were a big softy!"

Flapjack's eyes narrowed in Gwen's direction. "For your information, I was keeping her safe!"

"From what? Face masks and terrible rom-coms?" Gwen asked, barely able to contain another laugh.

"I was talking about her first date," he replied, swishing his tail.

Lizzie came around the corner before I could further question my self-appointed, pint-sized guardian. That was the other downside to having an assistant hanging around—it made talking to the ghosts nearly impossible without looking like a raving lunatic.

"Kimberly Gardner is on hold," Lizzie said, a nervous lilt to her voice as she held out the phone. "Line one."

"Ugh." I groaned as I took the phone. "What now? Let me guess—she's changing the order again? That would make it what … the fifth, no, *sixth* time? The wedding's in three weeks. How many times is she going to do this?"

Gwen gave me a pitying look as my finger hovered over

the illuminated button for a moment longer. Finally, I clicked onto the line.

"Hello, Kimberly. This is Scarlet. How can I help you?"

Silence greeted me on the other end.

"Kimberly?" I waited another beat and then put the phone back down and shrugged. "Guess she hung up."

Gwen looked past my shoulder and her expression darkened.

The bell on the front door jangled and my shoulders fell. I didn't need to turn around to know who had just wandered into the shop.

"I *tried* to call."

I slapped a serene smile on my face and pivoted on my heel. Kimberly stood, arms folded and one Louboutin tapping the welcome mat, with a sour look on her face. "I apologize, Kimberly. I was mid-design. What can I do for you today?"

"I've reconsidered my bouquet. The lilies would be a mistake," she said, pausing only to dig into her large purse and pull out a bundle of glossy bridal-magazine pages. She strutted across the shop and slapped them onto the counter. With dizzying speed, she flipped through the multitude of sticky-noted pages and stopped on a spread that showed a table loaded down with decadent centerpieces. "I think something like *this* is more ... *me*."

Gwen scoffed over my shoulder. "That's practically a carbon copy of the drawing you did two weeks ago!"

While I agreed whole-heartedly, I kept my smile buttoned up tight. I couldn't verbally agree with Gwen for a couple of reasons. First, because she's a ghost. Secondly, because Kimberly Gardner was a client. An incredibly important one. She was the first bride-to-be at the newly opened Lilac Bed and Breakfast, a historic home that I'd become entwined with a few months earlier. Let's just say there had been one

GHOSTS GONE WILD

seriously pissed-off ghost in residence during the renovation and without my help, the entire house would have ended up a crumbled heap of rubble. Thanks to my help with the spooky situation, I'd earned the exclusive right to provide florals for all events, including Kimberly Gardner's upcoming nuptials. Yay me?

Oh, and the whole thing was going to be on TV, adding another few degrees to the pressure cooker I found myself living in. The Lilac B&B's renovation had been featured on a popular home-improvement show, *Mints on the Pillows*, which resulted in a flock of bridezillas looking for a slice of the limelight when the show returned to film a special segment on the venue. Enter stage left: Kimberly Gardner.

She was by far one of the most demanding, entitled women I'd ever met, and thought for some delusional reason that her nuptials should be on par with something from the royal family across the pond. I honestly wasn't sure why she wasn't throwing her wedding in some kind of swanky Los Angeles hotel or on a tropical beach somewhere. Beechwood Harbor was a lovely town, tucked along the rustic Washington State coastline. Lush greenery collided with the majestic ocean, separated only by miles of sandy beaches. It was a beautiful place to have a wedding, but it wasn't quite up to the standards splashed through the newsstand's worth of bridal magazines that Kimberly was armed with 24-7. Rumor (Gwen) had it that Kimberly was a huge fan of the show and that her family had paid nearly triple the asking price to have her wedding be the christening event for the B&B's outdoor venue. To say the wedding was going to be over the top would be the understatement of the decade.

"Are you even *listening* to me?" Kimberly snapped.

My shoulder stiffened and I bit back the fiery retort on the tip of my tongue. Instead, I offered a placating smile. "Of course, Kimberly. I was making some mental notes, that's all."

"Well?" Her overly plump lips protruded into a duck pout. Had she had *more* work done since her last visit?

"I'm not normally a violent person, but this woman has me wishing I had the use of my hands," Gwen said, pantomiming a strangling motion at the woman opposite me.

"If I had the use of my claws, I'd join you," Flapjack said, jumping up onto the counter.

I rolled my eyes, only realizing a moment too late that Kimberly wouldn't understand why.

"Is there a *problem*?" she asked, crossing her arms.

"No, no, no," I said, scrubbing at my face. "My eyes are just really dry today. Allergies, you know? I should have put some eye drops in earlier."

Kimberly sighed. "You know what? I think I'm going to speak to Sonya again. This is clearly too much for you to take on right now and, as I'm sure you can understand, I really need someone with more experience handling my wedding florals."

Heat flashed over my skin and I planted my hands on the counter to keep them from shaking. I gritted my teeth but managed to hold onto what little patience I had left. I didn't want to kiss up to the woman, but she was a top-dollar client and my first bride with the Lilac B&B, an important business partner. So, it was time to pucker up. Just a little. "Kimberly, I'm going to make sure that you will be carrying the perfect bouquet when you walk down the aisle to become Mrs. Casper Schmidt."

Yeah, that's right. Her fiancé's first name is Casper. I nearly spit out my coffee when I'd taken the order.

My plan worked; Kimberly took on a certain glow anytime she heard the phrase *Mrs. Casper Schmidt*, and it tended to knock her down a few pegs below homicidal. The effect would strike me as adorable, perhaps even enviable, if she wasn't such a ginormous pain in my rear.

She'd plunked the magazines back on the counter and returned her attention to me. "It's all going to be fine." I picked up one of the glossy sheets from the counter. "Now, should I make a photocopy of this page, or may I keep it for reference?"

Kimberly's phone rang. She waved a finger, shushing me before ripping it from the outside pocket of her purse. "Where are you?" she barked without so much as a hello to the person on the other end.

She paused and her expression darkened.

"Oh boy," Gwen breathed, floating backward a few paces. "She looks like she's about to blow."

"That's not good enough, Drea! I *told* you I needed help today," Kimberly snapped. She spun on her high-dollar heels and stalked to the front window. "I'm giving you ten minutes. That's it!"

"Quick, Scarlet, hide anything pointy and sharp!" Flapjack warned.

"She is looking kind of ... *stabby*," Gwen added.

"Shush," I whispered, waving a hand at both of them. It was hard enough for me to keep up my unflappable routine without the pair of them hissing in my ears.

Kimberly ended her phone call with a snarl and slam-dunked her phone back to the depths of her beach-tote-sized purse. She turned back to face me and managed to find her smile, though it didn't quite reach her hazel eyes. The woman was nearly airbrushed perfection with a pulse. Everything from her skin to her glossy chestnut hair and her perfectly manicured fingernails was tended to and maintained. I had a feeling that the monthly receipts from her

DANIELLE GARRETT

boatload of beauty products would add up to more than I made in a quarter.

"As usual, she's late!" Kimberly fumed, her cheeks burnished with a color that had nothing to do with her bronzer. "Make a note of that: Drea is *not* allowed to be in charge of anything regarding the flowers. I'll make sure Sonya knows too—"

As if summoned, Sonya Perez, a striking woman with raven hair and olive skin, strode into the shop flashing a megawatt smile. "Good afternoon, ladies!"

How she maintained such a sunny disposition in Kimberly's near-toxic radius was beyond me.

"Hello, Sonya." The smile I offered her was genuine.

"Drea is late, as always," Kimberly complained. Her insufferable whine was like fingernails on a chalkboard.

"Don't worry. I've got everything under control." Sonya set a hand on Kimberly's forearm. "Now, what are these changes you're making? I simply can't wait to see what you come up with, Scarlet. Maurice has been raving about the designs you've been doing for the B&B guest rooms!" She peeked past me to my design table and spotted the arrangement I'd been working on before Kimberly barreled in. "Is that one of them? I simply *love* birds of paradise!"

Kimberly frowned, unhappy to be out of the center of attention.

"You're sure you can do this?" She eyed me, both of her painfully perfect brows drawn into sharp peaks.

"Ugh, give it a rest already!" Flapjack groused.

"I promise you, Kimberly, it will be beautiful. Okay?"

Before she could argue with me further, her phone rang. She plucked it out of her purse again and scowled. "It's Drea. Probably more excuses!" She answered the call and then reached for Sonya's arm. "I'll see you at the restaurant in one hour."

Without another word—never mind a thank you—she turned and stalked out.

"I'm really sorry about her," Sonya told me as soon as our shared little ball of sunshine was out of sight. Her bright smile faded and for the first time since meeting her six weeks beforehand, I realized that she was just as fed up with Kimberly's theatrics as I was. For some reason, that made me feel a little better.

Misery loves company, after all.

"It's fine." I handed over the magazine page labeled with three hot-pink sticky notes. "Here's what she wants now." I pointed at the design Kimberly had indicated before flipping to the next page. "We didn't get around to talking about either of these, so I'm sure they'll be her choice du jour tomorrow or the next day."

"Oh, goody," Gwen quipped.

"All right." Sonya nodded as she considered the image. "That works. Honestly, I don't know why she bothers to pay my fees. She doesn't even consult with me on these kinds of changes, just picks up the phone or fires off an email and I'm usually the last one to know what's actually going on."

I raised my brows. "Seriously?"

"Just last week, I chewed out the catering company for sending us the wrong quote for the second time, only to find out that Kimberly had been changing the menu behind my back." She shook her head. "So humiliating. Honestly, if it weren't for the absurd commission I'm set to make, I'd have bailed out months ago!"

"No wonder her sister avoids her at all costs," I said, my voice lowered.

"Oh, Drea is a whole *other* story," Sonya replied, adding an exasperated sigh. "Anyway, I know you're closing soon, so I'll get out of your hair and let you finish your work. We'll talk tomorrow, all right?"

"Works for me. Have a good evening."

Sonya waved as she headed out, and I returned to my studio.

Flapjack and Gwen followed, complaining about Kimberly's treatment of me for a few more minutes. They kept at it until Flapjack left to go revel in the stink wafting from the catch of the day as it was being cleaned down at the harbor docks.

"Enough about that horrible woman," Gwen finally declared when Flapjack was gone. "Let's talk about Lucas!"

Gwen had a semi-unhealthy obsession with my love life. Granted, she had the same fixation with nearly everyone in town; I was simply one of the few corporeals that she could talk to.

I returned to my studio and dove into work without commenting.

"You're really not going to tell me *anything*?" Gwen asked.

I slid a meaningful glance at Lizzie as she worked to print off a batch of inventory tags. Gwen huffed. "Fine, but I expect a full report on your romantic reunion first thing in the morning. Before the wrecking ball in a cardigan punches in for her shift."

Gwen's silvery silhouette shimmered and then vanished without a sound.

Somehow, Lizzie and I managed to squeeze the three outgoing orders into her clown car and I sent her off to deliver them before returning to my arrangement. For the first time in a long time, the studio was quiet. By the time Lizzie circled back near closing time, I'd rearranged the cooler, cycled out all of the old product, and cleared out the voicemail queue.

"How's tomorrow looking?" I asked Lizzie as she consulted the schedule on the front computer.

"Busy," she replied in an almost apologetic tone.

I sighed. "All right. Well the rental company said they would have a van available for me tomorrow morning, so I'll need you to run the show while I run over there to pick it up."

Lizzie nodded violently. "Of course!"

The front bell rang and she jumped up to go to the front counter, but I stopped her. "Why don't you go ahead and clock out since I'll need you early tomorrow."

"Okay. Have a good night, Scarlet. Thanks for everything."

She grabbed her purse and car keys from the office and slipped out the back door with a small wave. I went to the counter, eager to take care of the last customer so I could close up. Despite my cagey response to Gwen, I was looking forward to seeing Lucas again. More than I was willingly to admit. He was flying into SEA-TAC and making the three-hour drive into Beechwood Harbor in a rental car. He'd assured me that he would make it in time for a late dinner.

"Evening, sir," I said to the tall, lanky man standing at the front counter with an expectant look on his face. "How can I help you?"

"Are you Scarlet Sanderson?"

"That's right."

He reached up and rubbed his hand along the back of his neck. "I've never done anything like this before, but I need your help."

"Selecting the right flowers?" I asked, cringing because I already knew from his posture he wasn't there to pick up a bouquet.

"No, actually, it's about—well, it's about a ghost."

Of course it was.

CHAPTER 2

The man set a faded newspaper page on the counter. "I found your information from this article."

If there was ever a night to close up early, this should have been it.

I pushed the paper back to him and shook my head. "I'm really sorry, but I don't work with ghosts."

"But the article—"

"Is wrong."

"My ex-wife is haunting me."

A prick of curiosity needled at me. *No, no. Fight it, Scar. Remember what happened last time.*

"Strange things have been happening around my house ever since she died. I hardly ever go home now. She's always … there. Then, last week, I was driving to work and all of a sudden, my brake pedal wasn't working. I damn near crashed into a guardrail!"

I winced.

He reached for my arm. "I *need* help from someone who

knows what to do in a case like this, and according to this article, that's you!"

I wrinkled my brow. I couldn't walk away if he was in danger. "All right, fine! I'll see what I can do." I tugged my arm away. "But let's get something straight—I don't do exorcisms."

He tilted his head. "What is it you do then?"

"It's more like ... counseling."

The man barked a laugh. "Oh, you don't know Ruthie. She's stubborn as a mule! She's not going to listen to you ... or anyone, for that matter."

"With all due respect, I've been dealing with ghosts for the majority of my life. In my experience, an open conversation is enough to smooth over most unresolved issues."

He scoffed. "That won't be enough with her. She's a real piece of work—I used to tell her that she put the Ruth in ruthless." He laughed at his own joke then quickly realized I hadn't so much as cracked a smile. His smile faded and his expression turned stony. "I don't want a therapy session. I want her gone."

I folded my arms. "Let's say you live in Florida and one morning you go out for a swim, only to find a giant gator in your pool. You have two choices: call the people who trap gators and release them somewhere else or hire the people who will come shoot the poor thing. It's kind of the same thing with ghosts. I prefer to do the former. Catch and release, so to speak."

"Fine. I don't really care how you do it, Ms. Sanderson. Just so long as it works!"

I frowned. My clever analogy was completely wasted on the impatient man standing across from me.

With a sigh, I held up a hand. "As long as that's understood. I charge $500 for house calls."

I'd never seen someone write a check so fast.

Call me a sell-out, but hey, if I was going to spend my precious downtime chasing after a ghost, I was darn well going to get paid for it. Besides that, there was a good chance that if I added one more ghost to my already overflowing schedule, I'd lose my grip on what little sanity I had left. The fee was more like hazard pay.

"I'm Wilson Barnes. Just do what you have to do."

"I'll come out tomorrow after I close my shop. This is the correct address?" I pointed at the information on the check, noting the "Dr." in front of his name.

"That's the one."

"I'll see you tomorrow around six, Dr. Barnes."

"Thank you."

He hurried out of the shop, clearly ready to be done with his unpleasant errand. I slipped the check into the front pocket of my apron and locked the front door before heading upstairs to my apartment. I'd have to ask Gwen what she knew about the departed ex-Mrs. Barnes.

Hopefully it wouldn't be nearly as bad as he'd made it sound, but I learned long ago that asking 'what's the worst that could happen?' was just tempting fate.

∼

BY EIGHT O'CLOCK, my pending ghost adventure was the furthest thing from my mind as I paced in front of my front window. Lucas was on his way from the airport and my nerves were pitching toward an all-time high. Nearly three months had passed since the last time we'd seen each other. We met under odd circumstances when I'd found myself at the business end of his Taser. Not exactly the type of meet-cute you'd find on *The Bachelor*, but it was working for us so far. Lucas worked as head of security for *Mints on the Pillows*, the reality show that renovated what is now the

Lilac Bed & Breakfast, back in early spring. After we got past that whole move-and-I'll-taze-you thing, we realized we had a lot in common and started an unofficially official relationship. The only downside was that as soon as the renos were done, Lucas was off to the next city on the schedule. Since then, we'd managed to keep in near-daily contact: phone calls, texts, and an occasional video call. He'd offered, more than once, to fly me out to the set for a long weekend, but with everything ramping up at the flower shop—and good help being *so* hard to find—it hadn't worked out.

Which, I decided as I stood at the window nearly trembling, was both a blessing and a curse. In some ways, the anticipation of seeing each other was almost euphoric, but on the other hand, a nagging voice had starting casting doubt. What if the way I remembered Lucas was an illusion, some kind of construct I'd built up in my imagination? Or vice versa?

There was a possibility that the entire visit was going to tear apart the tiny threads of connection we had formed over the past months. I didn't want to watch it all unravel, but at the same time, the possibility that the bonds might tighten and root even deeper scared me more on some levels.

The tangled thoughts and doubts swirled around in my stomach as I waited at the window. After a few minutes, an unfamiliar car park in the lot below and I gasped out loud, excited that the moment was finally here.

Lucas emerged from the driver's side of the dark sedan and I smiled to myself as he straightened and stretched his long limbs. He was used to driving a burly pickup truck while on the set and the idea that he'd been folded into a tiny sedan for the past three hours, cursing the lack of legroom, made me giggle.

He glanced up and caught sight of me in the window, and

our eyes met. My heart did a series of gymnastics and then plummeted to my toes in a free fall at the smile he gave me.

"Is your gentleman caller here, Lady Scarlet?"

There was only one ghost in my life who would use the phrase "gentleman caller" and that was Hayward Kensington III, an old English gentleman who still clung to his sense of propriety more than a hundred years post-death. It was charming in a weird way. I nodded at him as I raised a hand to return Lucas's greeting. He crossed the lot and I jumped back from the window and scurried across the small apartment to stand post at the front door. Hayward followed and I belatedly noticed the downcast look on his face. "Are you all right, Hayward?"

"He's moping," Flapjack interjected, appearing at my other side.

Hayward's regal face twisted into a nasty scowl as he glared down at the unwelcomed presence. "Butt out, Flapjack!"

My eyebrows shot up. Hayward rarely used such language.

"Gwen's got herself a boyfriend," Flapjack said, his eyes almost glowing as he returned Hayward's stare.

"What?" I whipped around to face Hayward, ignoring the fuzzy specter at my feet.

Hayward removed his top hat and passed it back and forth. "It's true, Lady Scarlet."

"Are you sure? She hasn't said anything to me."

I glanced back at the front door. Lucas would be knocking on the other side at any moment. He knew about my ... *ability*, but I hadn't planned to spend our first night back together in some kind of ghost intervention to cheer up my longtime companion.

Flapjack wound around my ankles, tail swishing dangerously close to my skin. A cold breeze followed and sent a shiver up my back. I resisted the urge to kick out at his spirit. It wouldn't affect him and would only spread the chill through my body, but sometimes it was hard to hold back. "His name is Quinton. He's new in town."

"I haven't even heard about him," I told Hayward. "And believe me, Gwen tells me *everything*. Endlessly. If there was an Olympic medal for talking, she'd be a gold medalist ten times over."

Hayward smiled but it didn't reach his sad eyes. "She's waiting until tomorrow to tell you."

"Why?"

"She didn't want to intrude on your evening with Mr. Greene."

I sighed. Of course. She knew I was nervous about seeing Lucas again. Gwen was the kind of person who was always thinking about others, which somewhat explained her fascination with the town gossip and everyone's comings and goings. Part of it was sheer nosiness, but she was also a woman with a huge heart who went out of her way to help others in times of crisis. In case things went south with Lucas, she wouldn't want to have a blossoming relationship of her own to rub in my face.

"I shouldn't have said anything, Lady Scarlet." Hayward slid his hat back on, concealing his thinning silvery hair. "I only found out about this Quinton fellow day before yesterday. Gwen asked me to keep it a secret from you and I agreed but ..." He paused and his silver eyes went glossy.

A knock sounded at the same moment that Hayward vanished from sight.

I looked down at Flapjack, who dragged in an impatient sigh and said, "He saw Gwen and Quinton kissing in the park after she left the shop."

My heart clenched. Hayward had been admiring Gwen from afar since the moment we stepped foot into Beechwood

Harbor. I'd always assumed that Gwen secretly knew about his little crush but played coy so as to not make him uncomfortable. But suddenly I realized she may have been blissfully unaware the entire time.

A second knock dragged me from that sad possibility and I pulled the door open, barely remembering to smile.

Lucas wore his signature half-cocked grin but it faltered when his eyes swept over my face. "Hey?" He squinted. "Scarlet, are you all right? You look like you just saw a—" Lucas stopped short and our eyes locked together. "Well, *ghost*."

"Story of my life, pal," I snorted, and we both dissolved into laughter.

"Come in, come in," I said, still laughing. Lucas followed me over the threshold and I closed the front door behind him.

So much for a silver-screen reunion.

Lucas scanned the room, his hands in his pockets. "Safe to assume we have a third wheel tonight? Or maybe a fourth, fifth?"

I laughed and then dropped a meaningful look to Flapjack. "No. Actually. It's just us."

"Fine, fine," Flapjack said, twitching his tail as he strode for the door. "But if Hayward goes poltergeist, you'll know who to blame."

He slipped through the solid door before I could fire a retort at his fuzzy rear end.

Hayward was the least likely to go off the rails. His idea of a wild night probably used to run along the lines of staying up past eleven and having a second glass of port after dinner. Not much had changed since his death, though the port was no longer an option. Poor guy.

"How was the flight?" I asked, ready to move on from ghost talk.

"Can't complain," he replied. "At this point, I think I'm

more comfortable on a plane than in most of the hotel rooms I end up staying in."

I crossed the room and grabbed my beaded purse from the back of the couch. "Oh, come on now. The show isn't exactly putting you up in flea-bag motels."

Lucas chuckled. "You saying I'm spoiled?"

"Maybe a little bit," I teased, flashing a grin as I slipped the long strap of my purse over my shoulder and draped it across my hip. The colorful beadwork complimented the simple navy shift dress I'd paired with black leggings and a pair of stacked sandals. It was the girliest thing I'd worn since … well, since the last time Lucas had been in town. "You need to get back to your globe-trotting roots. A few days backpacking through the Amazon oughta fire up your sense of adventure."

"Not to mention make a three-star-hotel bed seem like a cloud straight from heaven."

I laughed. "Exactly."

"You know, I've actually been thinking it's about time for me to get back out there. I have the next couple of months off from the show. All I'm missing is a travel buddy." Lucas took a step closer to me and the temperature of the room seemed to jump ten degrees. He smiled down at me and brushed his fingers over the back of my hand. "You know anyone who might be interested in tagging along?"

My cheeks warmed and I ducked under the concealment of my copper hair that hung in loose waves, the result of a failed experiment with the curling iron earlier that evening. "As tempting as that sounds, I have a rampaging bridezilla who would probably go on a killing spree if I backed out of her wedding now."

It was a flimsy half-truth. In reality, I had a creeping suspicion that Kimberly would pop the cork off one of her ridiculously expensive bottles of champagne and throw a little party if I told her I was unavailable.

I tugged at Lucas's arm. "Come on, I'm starving."

He hesitated but then relented and followed me out of the apartment and down the back stairs to a small, residents-only parking lot behind the row of shops. We crossed the street and Lucas helped me into his rental car and we set off up the coastline. I didn't ask where we were going, opting to make small talk about the landmarks we passed on our way out of the small town instead. Twenty minutes later, we wound up at a fancy beach-side restaurant, dining on the moonlit back patio as the tide washed back in. Lucas didn't raise the proposal of traveling together again, but I couldn't stop thinking about it, which tainted the evening with a lingering heaviness.

"So, tell me, what kind of *spooky* escapades do you have planned for my visit?" Lucas teased as we started in on dessert. "Another murder mystery? Missing person? Haunted house?"

I glanced away and he tugged at my hand. He laughed. "Scarlet? I was just kidding."

"Well ... actually, there is this *one* thing."

Lucas groaned.

"Don't worry! It's just a little pit-stop tomorrow evening. I can totally handle it."

Lucas tilted his head, grinning at me. "I'm pretty sure that's what you said last time."

CHAPTER 3

"So, clearly, you can see why lake-stone blue for the ribbons is completely out of the question!" Kimberly droned the next afternoon.

Another day, another pseudo-crisis.

"Lake-stone blue?" Hayward repeated, looking in Flapjack's direction. "Is that a real color?"

Flapjack hitched one of his shoulders. "Apparently."

I shifted my eyes away from my companions and blinked. My eyelids felt like sandpaper. I'd stayed up way too late. If Gwen was around, she'd be begging and pleading for the details of my night out with Lucas, but oddly, she was nowhere to be seen. Unfortunately, Kimberly had burst through Lily Pond's doors mere moments after I'd unlocked them and launched into a tirade about her color scheme, wondering why I hadn't pointed out to her before that lake-stone blue clashes with the ivory of her dress. I was unaware that *anything* clashed with ivory, but she was insistent.

And loud.

So very, very loud.

Over the course of dinner with Lucas, I'd had a couple of glasses of wine and we'd ended up having a nightcap in his hotel room, which, as expected, was far above the two-star accommodations he'd made it out to be. I'd woken up slightly hungover and a little off my game.

Not that it would mean anything to Kimberly. I could be in traction at the hospital with pins and staples in every limb and she'd still find a way to march past the nurse's station to inform-slash-berate me on the changes she was making to her arrangements because my judgment was so poor.

I stared down at the swatches and samples she'd piled before me. With careful fingers, I plucked off the one labeled with the offending color. "I think the lake-stone blue works, but if you want something else, that's fine. I have an entire cupboard full of ribbons. We can find something you like."

Kimberly looked horrified. I might as well have reached over the counter and backhanded her perfect face.

"I'm not talking about the ribbons anymore! I'm *talking* about the vases!" She scoffed, gawking at me like I was the world's biggest idiot. "Honestly, I don't know *why* the producers are being so stubborn about using your services."

Hayward swooped in closer to my side, taking a protective posture. In reality, there was little he could do to help me, but it was comforting nonetheless.

I reached up and rubbed my temple, trying to stop my eye from twitching. "Right, right. Of course. It's not a problem. We can go with the ivory ones you liked at your first consultation."

Kimberly huffed and looked ready to start a new tirade when her phone rang. "Hello?" she barked into the slim phone.

I took a moment's reprieve as she spun around on her stilettos and continued her sharp conversation. "Yes, I'm *still* with the flower woman." She glared at me and then turned her back as if I was the one being rude.

"*Flower woman?*" Flapjack snarled.

Hayward shuddered. "I prefer to give people the benefit of the doubt, but this woman is simply reprehensible."

I rolled my eyes and nodded hard enough that my head started to throb again. Kimberly's voice rose and it became apparent that she was talking to her sister, Drea, again. "—don't care if you have to pay extra! Just make sure it gets here in time!"

I had no idea what she was ranting about—I was simply grateful that I didn't share DNA with the wretched woman.

Kimberly whipped back around, her face still pinched into a scowl. "Drea, stop whining! I have to go. Casper is on the other line." Without hesitation, she clicked off one call, and in the millisecond between answering the other, her face completely rearranged itself like a high-speed Rubik's cube, morphing from a nasty sneer to a bright, winner-of-the-beauty-pageant smile in half a heartbeat. "Casper, honey! Of course we're still on for breakfast, Shnookums. I'll be right there."

"That was creepy as hell," Flapjack said as her high-pitched greeting made us all flinch. "And that's coming from a ghost."

If it weren't for the emotional whiplash I'd just experienced, his wry comment would have likely reduced me to giggles. As it was, I wondered if I should tell Sonya to start slipping sedatives into Kimberly's tea. It couldn't be healthy to have a cord wound that tight—it was bound to snap eventually, and when it did, I hoped I was well outside the blast zone.

WHEN GWEN DID FINALLY SHOW up, it appeared that my date with Lucas and her own midnight tryst were the last things on her mind. Her eyes were wide with alarm as she surged through the front door and she kept her arms wrapped around herself.

"Lady Gwen!" Hayward was the first to speak. "Are you all right?"

Gwen shook her head and then her eyes locked on mine. "Scarlet, something terrible has happened."

I looked to Hayward and Flapjack. "What is it?"

"Last night, I was—" she paused, her eyes cutting to Hayward.

So she *did* know.

That was a quandary for another afternoon.

"I was out with a friend," she continued. "We ran into Myra—you know, Myra Marsh, everyone calls her M&M."

I nodded. "Of course I do."

Myra was a regular at our weekly support group. She'd been dead for fifteen years and still wandered Beechwood Harbor, in complete denial about what unresolved issues were keeping her from moving on to the other side. To everyone else it was obvious. She spent nearly twenty-four hours a day haunting her daughter's house at the edge of town.

They'd had an argument several years before and had stopped speaking to one another. The day Myra's car lost traction on a winding road and crashed through the guardrail into an ancient oak tree, the two were preparing to meet for lunch for the first time in years.

I'd offered to go and speak to her daughter, to tell her whatever it was Myra had been planning to say that day, but Myra always declined. After a few months, it became clear that for all her talk about moving on, she wasn't ready to leave. She couldn't hold her grandson or buy him a bike for Christmas, but she liked watching him grow up and didn't want it to happen without her, even though he had no idea she was there watching over him.

Gwen untucked her hand and flapped it. "Right, I don't know why I said that." She squeezed her eyes closed tight and then reopened them. "She said she'd been having weird spells. Moments where she would be standing in her daughter's kitchen watching her grandson, and then she'd lose time and wake up a few hours later not remembering what had happened."

"Wake up where?" I asked.

"Different places," Gwen said. "Once, she said she woke up in someone's attic. She'd never been to the house before and has no idea who lives there. She says she raced out as fast as she could. The next time, she woke up in the sporting equipment closet at the high school. Then, just two days ago, she says she woke up in the middle of the ocean, stranded in some kind of cave."

"And she has no idea how she got to any of those places?" I asked.

Gwen shook her head. "No idea."

"That is weird." I tapped a finger on my lips. "And she's always alone when she wakes up?"

"As far as I know," Gwen replied.

"Ghost sleepwalking?" Flapjack offered in a rare moment of helpfulness.

I shrugged one shoulder. "It's possible, I suppose. I've never heard of something like that before, but that doesn't mean it couldn't happen."

Naturally, ghosts don't need sleep, but that was the closest term for the deep meditative state of mind they could slip into. For some ghosts, it was simply a way to decompress or pass the time. Then there were ghosts like Gwen, who I was certain never took a moment away from the action. Even in the dead of night, she always seemed to have someplace to be, or, more likely, subjects to watch.

"I'll talk to her if you want," I offered. "Or she can bring it up on Sunday for the next meeting. Maybe someone else will have a better theory about what's going on."

"What if she disappears again before Sunday? Maybe she won't come back this time!"

"Gwen, hold up," I said, keeping my voice calm and soothing. "Let's not spin this out of proportion. I think it's weird, but it doesn't sound dangerous."

"No kidding," Flapjack interjected, twisting his nose as he looked up at Gwen. "What's the worst that could happen? She can't *die* again. Scar can't be everyone's Yoda. You're all lucky she tries at all!"

Gwen's eyes widened as they flew to me. "I'm sorry, Scarlet. I didn't mean to—"

I stopped her with an open palm. "It's all right. Flapjack is just feeling overly protective today."

Flapjack bristled.

"For good reason," Hayward said, chiming in for the first time. "That awful Kimberly woman was just here, raising a ruckus for poor Lady Scarlet." He shot Gwen a look as if to imply she should have been there to witness the exchange.

Gwen sighed. "Again?"

"Afraid so." I moved to the computer and pulled up the day's orders. In all of Kimberly's swirling chaos, I'd lost track of my usual morning routine. As the computer processed the batch of orders, I went to my small office and clicked on the miniature, four-cup coffee pot. The smell of rich, cocoa-infused coffee filled the air and I took a moment to breathe deeply and center myself before going back to the front counter. Lizzie would be arriving within a few minutes; she was accident-prone but delightfully punctual. I needed to sort out any lingering ghost business before she came crashing into the shop.

Gwen and Hayward stood at opposite ends of the front retail space, coolly ignoring one another. Meanwhile, Flapjack twitched his tail, amusement shining in his sapphire eyes as they bounced back and forth between them.

My heart broke for Hayward. I'd hoped that eventually Gwen would see his true feelings and come around to him. Sure, he may as well have been from a different planet than her, and was significantly older, both as a human and a ghost, but still.

I stuffed my disappointment down and offered a sunny smile in an attempt to brighten the mood of the room. "Gwen, while you're here, there's something I wanted to ask you about."

She turned around, a sly grin on her face. "What a coincidence—I had something to ask you too."

I groaned, already knowing where she was headed. "Let me guess, Lucas?"

"Bingo!"

Gwen deals in gossip, the juicier the secret, the higher the currency. If I wanted to know about the late ex-Mrs. Barnes, I was going to have to pony up.

"All right, fine. I'll tell you about last night, but first, what do you know about a Dr. Wilson Barnes? More specifically, his departed ex-wife Ruthie?"

"Ruth Barnes?" Gwen pulled a face. "Well, for starters, she's a total harpy!"

My heart sank. "Of course she is."

Gwen soared across the shop and took her usual perch on the counter. "Dr. Wilson is a respected OB/GYN who has a thriving practice one town over, but a large estate here in the Harbor. Ruth was a real shrew of a woman. Always accusing him of ogling other women, which was especially ironic, ya know, considering his job."

Hayward coughed and headed for the door. "This sounds like a private conversation," he said. "I'll return this afternoon, Lady Scarlet. Good day." He tipped his hat in my direction and then vanished.

Gwen's smile slipped from her face as she looked down at her folded hands. "He's angry with me, isn't he?"

I bit my lip.

"Ha! Ya think?" Flapjack burst out.

"Not helping," I told him as he launched up onto the counter and strutted along like he was on a—well, on a catwalk. "What happened between you two?" I asked, turning my attention to Gwen.

"Nothing! That was the whole problem."

I sighed. "Gwen, you know Hayward is from a different time. He's been around for a hundred years, but he's held fast to his old-fashioned manners. I mean, honestly, I don't know how many times I've told him that he doesn't have to call me *Lady* Scarlet. He insists. It's his way of showing respect."

"I know. I know." Gwen nodded and then sniffled. "I like him, Scarlet, I really do. I think it's adorable that he wants to be all proper. But I can't wait around forever."

Flapjack snorted and I shot him daggers across the room. "What?" he asked, feigning ignorance. "She technically literally *has* forever."

"That's not the point," I rebuffed.

Flapjack jumped down and stalked for the door, swishing his tail with each step. "Women."

I picked up an empty gift box and chucked it in his direction, the cardboard hitting the wall moments after he'd slithered through it. "Damn cat," I huffed. "I'm sorry about him, Gwen. If I could figure out how to get rid of him, I would."

She smiled through her silvery tears. "No, you wouldn't."

I ground my teeth, even as I had to nod in agreement. He drove me to the edges of my sanity nine days out of ten, but for whatever reason, I liked having him around.

"What do you think I should do about Hayward?"

I sighed. "Just give him some time and space. He'll rally and come back around."

"Will you talk to him for me?"

I wasn't sure what exactly I would say, but Gwen's pleading eyes were impossible to refuse, so I nodded. "Sure, sure. Of course, I will."

The printer fired off a series of pages and I took a beat to retrieve them. Gwen looked slightly more cheerful when I joined her at the counter. "What else do I need to know about Dr. Wilson and Ruthie?"

Gwen squared her shoulders. "They had a nasty divorce, mostly because she insisted on getting full custody of their two children. At the time of the divorce, their son was sixteen and their daughter was fourteen. She spread all kinds of rumors, trying to get people on her side. I'm not sure anyone listened, but it made for good popcorn drama." She paused and considered me. "Why are you so curious about Dr. Wilson all of a sudden?"

"Oh, right, I guess that was kind of random." I pulled my hair back into a low ponytail, preparing for the day's work. "He came in here last night right at closing time to ask me to help him get rid of Ruthie. He thinks she's haunting him."

"Is she?" Gwen asked.

I shifted my gaze to her. "Wouldn't that really be your area of expertise?"

Gwen giggled. "Fair enough. I actually didn't realize she was still hanging around. She died about a year ago."

"How long had they been divorced?"

"A few years. Separated a lot longer than that, but as I said ... nasty divorce. By the time the judge signed the papers, their son was eighteen and that part of the custody battle went away. It was a mess."

"Sounds like it." I shook my head.

"She stayed in town. Something about not wanting to make their daughter change schools when she was so close to graduation."

"Understandable."

"Yeah but it drove Dr. Barnes crazy."

"Why? You'd think he would be happy to be close to his kids."

"Oh, that part was probably fine. But Ruthie went a little ... overboard, shall we say, in flaunting her new divorcee status. She walked away with half his money, his prized sports car, and their second home in Aruba. She started dating younger men and wasn't shy about it." Gwen leaned in conspiratorially. "And then she got pregnant!"

My eyebrows spiked. "Oh?"

"Mmhmm. It was a huge scandal. Everyone was talking about it, mostly because she was forty-three and the father was twenty-two!"

"How did she die?"

"Car accident. She was on her way home from a long weekend away and swerved off the road. Luckily she hadn't picked up her baby from the sitter yet or he'd have been in the car too." Gwen shuddered at the thought.

"How awful." I cocked my head. "Any reason why she'd be haunting her ex? It sounds as though she'd moved on with her life, as brief as it may have been post-divorce. Why would she go back to him in death?"

Gwen shrugged. "I have no idea. Guess you'll find out. But a word of warning, Scarlet: she wasn't exactly what you'd call *stable* in life and if I had to guess, I'd imagine that's only gotten worse in death."

"Well that's a relief. It would be a real shame if I had to start dealing with sane ghosts. I'd have to start watching TV for entertainment or something."

CHAPTER 4

"All right, so what's the plan here?" Lucas asked as we idled outside the address printed on Dr. Barnes's check. Somehow he'd managed to sweet talk his way into accompanying me. I accused him of using his charm for nefarious purposes, which only made him laugh.

I glanced up at the massive house. Regardless of what the former Mrs. Barnes had walked away with in the divorce settlement, it was clear that the good doctor was still doing well for himself. The craftsman stunner was built atop a hillside that allowed a panoramic ocean view. We'd passed the nearest neighboring house on the way up the steep hill and I figured it was at least half a mile away, affording Dr. Barnes's residence tranquility among the trees. Then I remembered what he'd said about nearly being driven off the road and a pit formed in my stomach. If Mrs. Barnes's ghost was really behind the near-accident, she was one peeved spirit.

Yay. My favorite kind.

"We'll talk to Dr. Barnes and get a more detailed account of what's been going on," I shifted my glance away from the house to look at Lucas. Not for the first time, I wished we were anywhere but on a wild-ghost chase. There were plenty of other ways I would rather be spending the evening. "Most likely there is a time of day, or specific room of the house that he feels the presence of the ghost. We'll find her, see what she wants, and try to negotiate her departure."

Lucas cocked his head. "Easy enough, right?"

I laughed. "I would say it can't be harder than the fiasco with Rosie, but I don't want to jinx us."

Lucas had been my irritation-turned-partner in my last ghost caper. Sometimes, in reflection, I hardly believed that I'd been crazy enough to tell him about my strange ability in the first place. He'd been open to it and almost a little eager to learn the truth. In his time as head of security with *Mints on the Pillows*, he'd seen some strange things, so apparently my odd life wasn't too hard for him to swallow. Which either made him perfect for me, or bonkers. Maybe both?

"Good call." Lucas peered out his window. "Ready?"

I heaved a sigh. "As I'll ever be."

He chuckled and flung open his door.

Dr. Barnes welcomed us in—after checking his watch to confirm that I was on time. We stood in the foyer of the house and he gave Lucas a quick once-over.

"Dr. Barnes, this is Lucas Greene. He's my—" I stopped myself, realizing with a flurry of panic that I had no idea *what* he was. Assistant? Muscle? Hired help?

Or ... more terrifying ... *boyfriend?*

Lucas smiled and extended a hand to the doctor. "I'm Scarlet's friend. I like to have her back when she goes on house calls. Make sure everything's on the up and up."

Dr. Barnes shook Lucas's hand and offered a tight-lipped smile. "Great."

Lucas's quick save should have filled me with relief. It lifted the burden of labelling our status, but instead of being happy about it, a pang of disappointment bit into me. I dismissed it and forced a smile. There wasn't time to sit around dissecting my emotions or worrying about what the sharp stab in my chest might mean.

"Didn't you bring anything?" Dr. Barnes asked, returning his attention to me.

"Like what?"

"A kit of some kind? Instruments? Sage? How do you plan on getting rid of her?" He was clearly a man on a mission.

I held up a hand. "Dr. Barnes, please, as we discussed yesterday, we're doing this my way, okay? Now, where do you feel Mrs. Barnes's presence the most strongly?"

"*Ms. Jasson*," he corrected in an icy tone. "She kept the beach house but she didn't keep my last name. I saw to that."

Oy.

"Okay, right. Let's stick with Ruth. Where do you normally feel her? Have you ever audibly heard her?"

Dr. Barnes relaxed slightly and waved his hand toward the staircase to the right of the front door. "This way."

Lucas followed me as we ascended two flights of stairs to the third level of the house. We went down a hallway that ended with a set of double doors. Dr. Barnes opened them and we entered into what appeared to be his man cave though it was probably three times the size of most studio apartments. The walls were painted a dark forest green and shadowboxed frames, each containing a signed jersey from some sporting team, were hung precisely six inches apart on one entire wall. I never paid much attention to sports, but the collection must have been impressive, as Lucas let out a low whistle.

I rolled my eyes and then turned to take in the rest of the room. A sprawling wet bar complete with a full-size fridge, sink, and three different brews on tap. Three long leather couches formed a u-shape in the middle of the room, opposite a TV that had to be bigger than the one down at the local movie theater. A popcorn machine sat at an angle in the corner beside a few arcade games and a pool table with custom felt that displayed the same logo as the jerseys.

"This is where you feel Ruth?" I asked, wondering if we'd taken a wrong turn. In a house this size, maybe that was something that happened? Or, maybe he'd just wanted to show off his collection.

Dr. Barnes pocketed his hands. "The TV goes on the fritz every time I have the guys over. The arcade machines too. And don't get me started on the popcorn machine."

Lucas raised his eyebrows as we exchanged a quick glance.

"What happened with the popcorn machine?" I asked.

I couldn't help it. It was too odd *not* to.

"I haven't used it for six months. The last time I turned it on, the thing kept popping and popping. By the time I managed to shut it off, there was three inches of popcorn all over the floor!"

I blinked hard, wondering if I'd heard him right. "How—I mean, that doesn't even seem possible. Where would all of the kernels have come from?"

Dr. Barnes narrowed his eyes. "I paid you $500 to figure it out. She's here. Somewhere. Some way."

I shook my head. "Well, for the moment, she's not. There aren't any ghosts in here."

Dr. Barnes threw his hands into the air. "Search the whole house. I don't care what it takes."

He stormed from the room before I could fire off any further questions. When the sound of his angry footsteps faded, I slowly pivoted on the heel of my sneakers to look at Lucas. Of course, he was busy getting up close and personal with every encased jersey that hung on the wall. He turned to glance at me, his face like a little boy on Christmas, and jabbed his thumb at the glass before him. "Scarlet, do you see this?"

"I do, but I gotta be honest—it doesn't mean anything to me. I don't even know what I'm looking at. Football? Basketball?"

Lucas's jaw dropped again. A series of sputters came out but he was apparently too appalled to find actual words.

"Okay, I get that this is like man heaven, but we have a ghost to find, all right?"

He followed, begrudgingly, as I began the search. After a quick sweep of the third floor, we moved to the second. Dr. Barnes had retreated to a lavish study and all I dared was a quick peek inside before moving to the next room. Finally, I spotted her down in the kitchen.

Ruthie Jasson, formerly Barnes, stood in the kitchen, elbows propped on a granite-covered island that was longer than my delivery van, staring wistfully out the picture windows that lined the opposite wall. She didn't tear her gaze away even as I said her name.

"Ruthie? Is that your name?"

She sighed. "Will always complained about my cooking, but I'm telling you, I made some truly beautiful meals right here in this kitchen, all while watching my babies play in the backyard."

I looked over my shoulder and gave Lucas a nod.

His eyes went wide as they swept the room. He couldn't see or hear Ruthie but that didn't stop his natural curiosity from trying.

"Ruthie, do you know why I'm here?" I asked, moving a little closer to the woman.

She was classically beautiful: a heart shaped face with high cheekbones, full lips, and large eyes. Though she shimmered slightly when she moved and was reduced to a monochromatic silvery-purple, it was clear that her final outfit—a form-fitted dress that showcased hours of work in the gym and a strict diet—had been pricey. Her long hair was pulled back in a sleek chignon at the base of her neck and held in place with a shiny clip of some kind. Personally, I'd never mastered much beyond a ponytail or topknot in the hair-design department. I could arrange a dozen roses into an artful bouquet but when it came to my hair, I was a lost cause.

Ruthie looked up at me and sighed again. "Will is tired of playing our little game and wants me out of his house."

I blinked. "That's right."

She pushed up to her full standing height, a few inches shorter than my own five-six frame. Her eyes drifted past me and locked onto Lucas. "Ooh, who is *that*? If you brought him as a distraction, consider it mission accomplished. I'd be happy to haunt him any day of the week."

"No!" I said, a little *too* emphatically.

Lucas straightened and I held out a hand, silently telling him *at ease*.

"You're not going to haunt anyone," I told the woman.

Ruthie's expression shifted, the serene, almost dazed look disappearing in an instant. "Is that so? What are you going to do? Exorcise me?"

"That's not what I do."

She smiled. "Then it seems my position is safe."

I folded my arms. "What is it that you want, Ruthie? Something tells me that you have a price."

Women like her always did.

Jeez, I've been listening to Flapjack too much. Apparently, his jaded worldview was transferrable.

Ruthie mirrored my posture and met my firm stare with one of her own. "I want Will to send my alimony money to my son, Damon."

I cocked my hip. "I'm not exactly a divorce expert, but I would think alimony payments would stop when you—"

"Dropped dead?" Ruthie snapped. "Technically yes, but Old Moneybags up there has plenty to go around. I was counting on that money for my son's schooling and future endeavors. Without it, he might have to ... well, I shudder to think it, but he might have to go to *public school*."

"Oh, good grief."

"What's she saying?" Lucas asked.

"She wants money. Would you mind getting Dr. Barnes so we can get these negotiations underway?"

Lucas gave a nod and headed back toward the stairs off the kitchen nook.

I turned my attention back to Ruthie. "And if he says no?"

"Well, until he agrees, I'll be here, breaking up boys' nights and if he so much as *thinks* of bringing a date back here, he'll see what I can really do. And I can assure you, it will be a lot less pleasant than some spilled popcorn on his plushy Berber carpet!"

"Just simmer down." I scoffed and turned away from her.

Dr. Barnes and Lucas appeared moments later. The good doctor's casual swagger must have evaporated during the walk because his face had gone a bit green and he shifted from foot to foot as he stood considering the kitchen. "She's —she's here?" he said, barely above a whisper.

I gestured at Ruthie for reference. "She wants you to continue her alimony payments. She wants the money sent to ensure that her son, Damon, has a secure future."

Dr. Barnes barked a sharp laugh. "So, in addition to being dead, she's also lost her mind!"

Ruthie puffed up her chest and levitated a few inches off the floor, bringing her to my eye level. "You tell that *warthog* of a man that he has a week to comply, or the next time his car goes a little *squiggly* it's going to be a far bumpier ride!"

GHOSTS GONE WILD

"Her bastard of a son isn't my problem. She should have thought of him before she defaulted on the payments for the beach house in Aruba. She could have sold that and had more than enough money for her snot-nosed little brat."

"How *dare* you!" Ruthie screamed. The sound vibrated off the glass but Lucas and Dr. Barnes's expressions remained unchanged. They hadn't heard the ear-piercing cry.

Dr. Barnes scoffed. "Why can't her stripper-turned-bartender boyfriend pay for him?"

"Dr. Barnes, if you don't … mind … my—" I squeezed my eyes closed against the high-pitched shriek as Ruthie began swirling through the room like a ghost tornado. "Ruthie!"

She stopped screaming and landed on the top of the island, glowering down at all three of us.

I drew in a breath and willed the residual ringing to stop. "Dr. Barnes, it's none of my business, but it seems it would be easier to write her son a check than to let this continue."

"She's not getting a penny," he replied, his jaw so tense I worried he was doing muscular damage. His eyes darted around. "How do I know she's really here? What if this is all some scam? You're going to tell me the address to send the money and I'm supposed to trust it will go to that woman's son?"

"What?!" I whipped my head around, shocked at the sudden turn. "You do realize that *you're* the one who asked *me* for help? It's not like I'm hoofing it door to door selling exorcisms and carpet shampoos."

Lucas snorted.

"This was a mistake. All of it." Dr. Barnes huffed and threw a hand toward the arched entry into the kitchen. "Just leave!"

"Gladly!" I said, stalking back toward the front of the house. "Enjoy your hauntingly ever after!"

"Can you believe that jerk?" I asked Lucas, throwing the passenger door of his rental car open minutes later.

Lucas buckled himself into the driver's seat. "Look at it this way—he's the one who's going to have to figure out how to get all that butter out of his carpet."

"Oh, the trials of the wealthy." I feigned a swoon and we both cracked up. "Can you imagine? A whole *sea* of popcorn?"

I shook my head and then wiped at my eyes, dabbing away the tears from laughing so hard. "I seriously want to know how she does it. It must be like one of those ball pits they have for kids. Except with butter ... so much butter."

My phone's ringtone interrupted and I dug into the bottom of my purse to retrieve it. "Wonder if that's him," I said, flipping it around to face me. The theory was instantly dispelled as I cringed at the caller ID on my phone. "Not Dr. Barnes. It's Sonya."

"Who's Sonya?" Lucas asked.

"Bridezilla's wedding planner."

Lucas grabbed the phone from my hand and chucked it back into my purse. "Sounds like she can wait. There'll be no worrying about fire-breathing bridezillas on my watch."

It was hard to argue with his logic, especially considering the steamy kiss that followed.

∼

THE STUDIO SPACE beneath my apartment was still dark when I descended the stairs the following morning. I'd gotten in late—really late—and hadn't seen anyone, not even Flapjack, when I got home.

"Morning. Gwen? Hayward?" I called out into the dark studio space as I hurried to turn on the lights. "Is anyone here?"

A voice called back after a few moments and sent my heart into a frantic beat. "Yes, *someone* is here!"

Kimberly? How the hell did she get in here?

I flicked on the lights over the counter and my jaw hit the ground.

Kimberly Gardner was indeed standing in my shop, but there was something different about her: mainly, she was dead.

CHAPTER 5

"Ki—Kimberly?" I stuttered, trying to wrap my brain around the silver-silhouette version of the woman who'd single-handedly doubled my wine budget ever since she blew into town. "What—what happened? You're—"

"Dead?" She gave a haughty flip of her hair. "Yeah, I've been informed of that."

I staggered forward and braced my hands on the counter, needing something solid to lean against. I couldn't stop staring at her. She was wearing the same sundress she'd been wearing the morning before when she'd ripped into me for not pointing out the snafu in her color scheme.

"What the hell happened to you?" Eloquence before coffee was a rarity in my world on even the best of days.

"I don't know," she replied quietly, showing the first sign of anything less than pure bravado and firepower. "I woke up this way, right there in my hotel. I thought it was a strange dream. I saw a double of myself sprawled across the bed."

"You don't know how you died?"

She shook her head. "Someone knocked on the door,

loud. The next thing I knew, there were paramedics, fire fighters, hotel staff, and police officers swarming the room. They shoved Casper right out of the room. I tried to talk to him, to any of them—but they couldn't see me."

She fell silent, her eyes roving unfocused past my shoulder for a few moments. "I tried to wake up. I tried so hard. But it just ... wouldn't work."

"I'm so sorry, Kimberly. That's—well, it's awful."

A sharpness returned to her eyes as they shifted back to meet mine. "You have to help me. I can't be dead. This isn't how this was supposed to go!"

A silver streak burst through the front door.

"Scarlet! I just heard the craziest—" Gwen stopped abruptly, her eyes locked on Kimberly. "Thing."

"Who are you?" Kimberly demanded, giving Gwen a disapproving once-over.

"Um—I'm Gwen."

"Gwen, huh? Missing a tambourine, aren't you?"

Gwen's eyebrows surged up her smooth forehead. "*Excuse* me?"

Kimberly hitched a shoulder. "Tambourine, crown of daisies, something."

I slammed my fists onto my hips and glared at Kimberly. "Listen up, this is *my* shop and Gwen is *my* friend. You will not speak to her that way! Or to any of my other friends, for that matter."

As if summoned, Hayward and Flapjack floated in through the wall.

Kimberly's lip curled back as she looked at them. "What kind of house of horrors are you running here?"

Hayward was stunned into silence. Flapjack, on the other hand, looked positively delighted. "Well, well, well. This is a fun surprise. I see someone finally gave you a dose of your own nasty medicine. I hope it was painful."

I drew in a slow breath. "Flapjack, please?"

His sapphire eyes shifted to me, then to Kimberly and back again before he gave a slight nod and sat back on his haunches. He'd back down—for now.

"What are you even doing here, Kimberly? I'm really sorry that you're ... gone, but surely I'm not at the top of your list for potential haunting victims."

Kimberly turned away from the stand-off with Flapjack. "I was told that you could help me. Apparently in addition to sub-par flower arrangements, you have some kind of Day-of-the-Dead side business going on here."

I narrowed my eyes and made a conscious decision to ignore the snarky jab at my designing skills. "I can try. What is it that you need?"

"I want my body back. Duh!"

A startled laugh burst from my lips. "What? Oh, no, no! I do *not* mess with that kind of stuff. Necromancy is not even close to being on my radar. Not now. Not ever."

Kimberly frowned. "Then what use are you? Why would that woman—ghost—*thing* send me here?"

"I don't know who sent you, Kimberly, and I'm sorry if there was some kind of confusion, but I—"

"You have to do something!" Kimberly pressed, surging closer to me. She moved with stiff, almost jerky motions. New ghosts often took a little time to adjust to their new form. "I can't be dead! I'm engaged! I was just starting my life."

Regardless of my feelings toward the woman, it was hard to watch her struggle.

"Like it or not, cupcake, this is your new life," Flapjack told her, not one ounce of compassion in his tone. "We're all dead. Well, except for Scarlet. You think any of us *wanted* this? Of course not! It happens. You adjust. Coming in here complaining and demanding things isn't going to get you anywhere but banished!"

"Flapjack..."

"Banished?" Kimberly repeated, her eyes darting back to mine. "If you can do something like that, then you obviously have powers! Now put me back. I'll give you anything you want as soon as I get into my body again."

"Kimberly, please. You have to try to understand." I softened my tone. "I can't change what's been done. If there is something I can do to help you adjust to your new life, I will. But that's the limit of my power."

"Worthless!" Kimberly snapped, turning away. A gust of chilly air whipped behind her.

A silver shimmer caught the corner of my eye and I turned just as Ruthie Jasson sailed through the wall. Her eyes zeroed in on me like a pair of heat-seeking missiles. Was it really too much to ask the universe to wait until I was caffeinated? "There you are!"

"When it rains, it pours," I sighed as I cast a miserable glance at Gwen and Hayward. At least Lizzie wasn't scheduled to come in until after noon. There was no way I'd be able to ignore all of this long enough to get any work done. "What are you doing here, Ruthie?"

"I'd think it would be fairly obvious," she answered, folding her arms. "You've got to get that cheapskate to agree to turn over the alimony money. If he doesn't get into the right preschool, his entire life could be over before it even starts!"

"Who is *this*?" Kimberly snapped, glaring at Ruthie. "Actually, it doesn't matter. Listen, lady, I was here first. So whatever your problem is, you're going to have to wait your turn!"

I held up my hands. "Actually, you're *both* going to have to wait your turn. I have work to do. *Real*, pay-the-bills work. I'm sorry, but I don't have time for either of you right now.

You can come back Sunday evening at seven-thirty. That's when I have office hours, so to speak."

Both frantic women started arguing with me, their high-pitched voices blending into one screechy roar.

Flapjack hissed but it didn't do any good, he was drowned out by the chaos.

"Okay, I very rarely do this, but you've both gotta go." I reached under the counter and retrieved a small iron bar I kept there for desperate times. Kimberly and Ruthie didn't even realize I'd said anything to them; both were too busy complaining and arguing. Ruthie spotted the iron bar and opened her mouth, likely ready to spew another grating remark, but I was quicker. With a swish of the bar, she vanished with a *whoosh* sound. Kimberly's eyes went wide and I whipped the bar through her silhouette too, wincing as she disappeared. "I'm sorry," I told the remaining spirits with a cringe.

"Scarlet!" Gwen squawked. "What did you do?"

I put the bar away. "Dispersed them."

"What does that even mean?" she asked, searching the room with frantic eyes.

"They'll both reset to where they died. It's disorienting, but I promise they're not hurt in the process."

"You're sure you didn't … *kill* them?" Gwen ventured, peeking between her fingers.

"Gwen, they're already dead!"

"Right, right." She nodded but didn't look convinced.

I massaged my temples and let my eyes slide closed for a moment. "I needed a second to think, and I'm pretty sure we can all agree that wasn't going to happen with the two of them around."

"Quite right, Lady Scarlet. I haven't heard such a commotion since The Great War."

"You were in a war, Hayward?" Gwen asked.

GHOSTS GONE WILD

"Well, not *in* the war, but the effects were felt at every doorstep."

Their conversation was ridiculously off topic, but I let it slide. At least they were talking to each other again.

"Your little trick won't hold them off for long," Flapjack said, ignoring Hayward and Gwen's side chatter.

"I know," I replied. "But I've got work to do. I don't have the time or energy to deal with either one of them right now."

"I wonder who whacked the witch," Flapjack mused, entirely too pleased over the whole thing."

I shot him a scowl. "I don't know. Sonya must know what's going on. In fact, she called me last night."

"Oh?" Flapjack said. "About what?"

"I don't know. I was with Lucas and we were—" I stopped as Gwen's ear perked. She spun around to face me, a wide, expectant smile on her face. "Anyway, the point is that I didn't answer. I figured it was something about Kimberly, but I never imagined she was calling to tell me she was dead!"

"We need to figure out what happened."

Gwen came closer. "That's what I was coming to tell you!"

Hayward joined us, his war-era tales packed away for another day. "You know what happened, Lady Gwen?"

"Not exactly. There are a few stories going around town. Most people are pegging it on the fiancé. You know it's always the husband or boyfriend!"

"That's not true," I replied, frowning. "Look what happened last time we assumed that."

We all took a beat of stilted silence, remembering Rosie, the ghost who had given all of us a run for our money a few months before.

I drew in a breath and shoved aside the memory. "How did she die? Let's start there."

"No one knows for sure," Gwen answered. "She was

found in her hotel room. She'd tried to call 911, but she was already dead by the time the paramedics got there and located her room."

"I'll call Sonya," I said, reaching for the phone.

I was still dialing when Lucas backed through the front door, a large coffee cup from Siren's Song in each hand. "You would not *believe* the line over there! How is there only one coffee shop in this whole town?" He chuckled to himself and then turned away to let the door slowly swing closed. He walked right in between Gwen and Hayward, oblivious to the somber, and yet chaotic, scene he'd entered into.

"Here's your hazelnut—" He froze, one cup extended toward me. "Are you okay?"

I had a feeling that was going to be a frequent question over the course of our relationship.

"Kimberly, the bridezilla I told you about? She was found dead in her hotel room last night. I'm calling Sonya, the wedding planner, to find out what happened."

Lucas swore under his breath. "The one who called you last night?"

I nodded and waited for the call to connect.

"Hello?" Sonya's voice sounded muffled and far away. She likely hadn't gotten much sleep.

"Sonya? It's Scarlet, over at Lily Pond Floral Design. I just heard the news."

"Oh, Scarlet, thank you for calling. I'm working through notifying everyone involved with the wedding plans. Canceling events is something I'm familiar with, but as you can imagine, this isn't exactly the usual reason weddings go belly-up."

"I'm sorry I missed your call last night."

"Oh! Don't worry about it. I was going to see if Drea could stop by your shop and pick up a few flowers."

I blinked, the puzzle pieces in my mind shifting into a new configuration. "So, it wasn't about Kimberly?"

"Yes and no." Sonya drew in a sigh. "We had a little bit of a fiasco with the cake tasting. Long story short, I was having some cake samples sent to her hotel room last night in a last-ditch effort to nail something down. I was going to see if I could have Drea run over to get a couple of flowers to garnish the samples. Kimberly wanted to make sure the flowers wouldn't affect the taste of the cake." Sonya sighed again and muttered something that sounded like, *ridiculous woman*, on the exhale.

"In the end, it didn't matter. I don't even think she ate the samples. Drea offered to take the samples to the hotel for me since she and Kimberly and Casper were supposed to get a later dinner together. I was just glad I wouldn't have to see Kimberly again." Sonya stopped herself. "I'm sorry, Scarlet. You must think that I'm horribly unprofessional and callous. I'm sad that she's suffered such a tragic fate, but I can't say I'm sorry to lose her as a client. She was a nightmare to deal with, as I'm sure you know."

"Well, I—um, she was ... *unique*."

Sonya laughed. "You really are an angel, aren't you?"

I nibbled my lower lip. I wasn't about to repeat some of the less-than-savory thoughts I'd had about Kimberly in the weeks since her initial consultation. But let's just say they were far from cherubic.

"Do you know what happened to her?" I asked.

"No," Sonya replied. "Drea called me this morning to tell me the news and I've been making phone calls for the last couple of hours. She said she went to the hotel last night to drop off the cake samples but bailed before dinner because the not-so-happy couple was arguing and she didn't want to listen to it."

"Oh?" My eyebrows hitched up my forehead.

"That was a fairly common thing," Sonya continued. "Casper and Kimberly were one of the least compatible couples I've ever worked with. I keep my lips buttoned in situations like that, but it was difficult with them. I wanted to take Casper aside many times and tell him to run for his life."

"Yikes."

"I don't mean to be cruel—"

"I understand. Listen, my other line is buzzing," I lied. "As far as the wedding, I'll refund the security deposit to the family as a goodwill gesture."

"Actually, they were wondering if you could put it towards funeral arrangements. They've decided to hold the funeral here in town at the Lilac House, since Kimberly was so fond of it."

"Oh. Um, yes, of course."

"Great. Two birds, one stone. I'll give you a call later to go over the details once I've talked to the family. Her parents are flying into Seattle a little later today." The lack of compassion in Sonya's voice was starting to disturb me. Sure, I wasn't a prime member of the Kimberly Gardner Fan Club, but I wasn't able to sweep aside her death as easily as Sonya. Then again, it might be easier for her, seeing as how she didn't have Kimberly's ghost barging into her morning-coffee routine.

CHAPTER 6

It didn't take long for Kimberly and Ruthie to find their respective ways back to my front door.

Four hours and seventeen minutes, to be precise.

Ruthie arrived seconds ahead of Kimberly, mad as a wet hen, hissing threats at me if I didn't get her ex-husband to come around to her side. I had the iron in hand when Kimberly popped back in, screaming louder than a banshee —or, at least what I imagined a banshee would sound like. I'd never had the displeasure of meeting one before.

The best part of the pissed-off-ghost brigade was the fact that Lizzie had punched in for her shift, rendering me mute. At least to the ghosts. That left Gwen, Hayward, and Flapjack to run interference for me.

"Ladies, *please*, one at a time!" Hayward called out over the squawking women. I'd never heard him yell before, but I had a feeling he was about three minutes from throwing his propriety right out the window if the pair of histrionic divas didn't put a sock in it.

"My problem is a little more important than this ... this ... cougar wannabee!" Kimberly shouted in reply, shooting daggers in Ruthie's direction as they squared off on opposite sides of my worktable. "I mean, really—a baby at *your* age?"

"Not that it's any of your business, but he's not a baby anymore," Ruthie said, snarling back at Kimberly. "He's three and it's imperative that he's accepted into a good preschool!"

"Ugh. Scarlet doesn't have time to worry about your walking mid-life crisis's preschool arrangements. She has to get my body back!"

The scream I was suppressing burrowed deeper and deeper, and I knew that when I finally snapped, it was going to be a window-breaker.

"Let them tear each other to pieces," Flapjack interjected, floating up to sit at my side as I tried to work on a large arrangement that needed to be ready for pick-up in less than half an hour. "Saves you the trouble once we get blondie out of here." He jerked his chin at Lizzie's back as she hummed away, blissfully unaware of the rampaging ghosts standing right behind her.

"Scarlet told you she will help you, but you have to come back on Sunday night. That's when we hold our meetings," Gwen said, her voice a soothing sing-song tone. Moments like these, I realized she'd missed her calling as a kindergarten teacher.

"Oh, butt out, hippie!" Kimberly snarled.

Okay. That's enough. I threw my shoulders back and cleared my throat. "Lizzie? Would you mind running this out to the delivery van?" I asked, tying a large bow around the glass vase containing a spray of blooms and greenery. It wasn't my best work, but considering I had five ghosts in a tangled war of words, it wasn't bad either.

"Sure," Lizzie replied, turning around to face me. "Do you want me to do the delivery?"

"No!" Gwen, Flapjack, and I all shouted in reply. She could only hear my voice, but the effect was still enough to

GHOSTS GONE WILD

make her wince. A pang of guilt surged through me. "Sorry, I'm just a little on edge today. A little drive will do me some good. Thanks, though."

Lizzie still looked hurt when she reached out to take the vase from me. I watched, a small frown on my lips, as she gingerly carried it out the back door with a determined expression.

As soon as the metal door clicked shut, I whipped around, waggling my finger at the two intruders. "Listen up! You two are going to leave me alone. I will not stand here listening to you complaining and fighting all day. Kimberly, I already told you—you're dead. There's no body recovery. No second chance. This is it. Got it? Dead. The end." I rounded on Ruthie. "And you—there's nothing I can do. I tried talking to your ex, he said no. I can't hack into his bank account and steal the money and I can't reach into his brain and change his mind, so we're at an end, too."

I stalked to the cash register and grabbed the iron bar. I brandished it at the two ghosts. "I'm very sorry. I wish I could help, but I can't. Now, either you leave on your own volition, or you're getting whacked. Either way, you're going!"

"Geez," Ruthie said, looking at Kimberly. "Is she always like this?"

Kimberly gave a bored shrug. "I think she's deeply unhappy. I've never seen her smile. She needs a man."

"Argh!" I lurched toward her with the iron but she vanished seconds before I could disperse her.

Ruthie rolled her eyes and gave a *harrumph* before she too vanished.

Hayward burst into applause. "Bravo, Lady Scarlet!"

I shoved the iron bar back into its hiding place and then raked my hands through my hair, roughly tying it back in a ponytail. "Thank you. Now, if you'll all excuse me, I have a delivery to make."

～

Lucas and I sat at my consultation table, enjoying an early dinner he'd brought over from the local pub when Sonya and Drea stepped into the shop. Lizzie had gone home for the day—without breaking anything—and so far, Ruthie and Kimberly were leaving me in blessed peace.

"Hello, ladies," I said as the front door swung closed behind them. I dabbed my lips with a napkin and wiped the french fry grease from my fingertips before jumping up from my place at the table.

"Sorry to interrupt," Sonya said with an apologetic frown. "Drea's parents just got in and wanted us to come over and get the order placed for the flowers. They want to hold the funeral two days from now."

I blinked. "Oh. Wow. That's fast."

"They don't want to be in town any longer than they have to," Drea responded. She was so different than her flashy big sister. Where Kimberly was boisterous, loud, and borderline obsessed with her looks, Drea was slight, quiet, and kept most of her pretty face hidden behind a curtain of dark, almost black, hair.

"I'm so sorry for your loss, Drea. Kimberly was a really special woman."

Flapjack snorted and Gwen shushed him loudly.

"Thank you," Drea replied.

Lucas stood up and started to clear the table, throwing all the wrappers and napkins back into the brown paper bag. "I'll get this out of your way," he said, swiping away some crumbs.

"Thanks, Lucas. I'll see you tonight?"

He nodded and shot a quick, muted smile at Sonya and Drea before slipping past them and out the door.

"Here are the details for the funeral arrangements." Sonya handed over a page torn from a pastel-pink legal pad. "Will that work?"

I glanced over the paper. Sonya was an event pro. She knew the types of flowers and foliage that a florist was most likely to have on hand. I'd need a few things from the floral market, but it was doable.

Drea stepped over to the table and started rummaging in her purse. Moments later, she came up with a checkbook. "I can write you a check for the difference."

I reached out and set my hand on her arm. "Please, don't worry about it. The security deposit will be more than enough. I'll be sure to leave an itemized statement with the delivery. Along with a refund, if applicable."

"Thank you, Scarlet. But don't worry about a refund. I know how many hours you've likely put into this already." Drea tucked the checkbook away. "Sonya, I think I'm going to head back to the hotel."

"Of course. I'll see you back there a little later this afternoon. I just have a few more errands to run."

Drea and I exchanged goodbyes and she left the shop.

"Poor thing," I said, releasing a heavy sigh as the doorbell jangled after her.

"It's a nightmare," Sonya agreed. "Her parents are just as pushy and demanding as Kimberly. It's a wonder Drea ended up being so *normal*."

"Any word on what happened to Kimberly? No one seems to have a solid story."

Gwen had flown in and out of the shop half a dozen times over the course of the morning, each time returning with a different hypothesis as to how Kimberly had met her end. Of course, for Gwen, the theories and speculations were her favorite parts. I was more concerned about the immediacy of whether or not there was some looming boogeyman hiding in the shadows, attacking women in their beds.

Sonya eyed the vacant table. "You mind if we sit?"

"Not at all."

She took a seat and immediately kicked out of her sky-high heels and began rolling her ankles in small circles. "The details are still coming in, but it seems she had some kind of allergic reaction. An attack, really. As Drea said, it appears Kimberly and Casper had an argument. He left to get some air. She stayed behind in their hotel suite. She ate something that didn't sit well and by the time she realized what was happening, she was puffed up so badly that she couldn't even speak. She called 911 but she was impossible to understand. She made it out into the hallway and one of the maids recognized the symptoms and got one of those epinephrine pens. But it was too late. By the time the police got there, she was gone."

I shuddered as the chilling words painted a gruesome picture in my mind. "Poor Kimberly," I breathed.

"It's all pretty awful. Casper came back as the paramedics were trying to revive her."

Across the room, Gwen made a gulping sound. I twisted slightly in my chair and saw that she was sobbing into Hayward's shoulder.

I shook my head as I turned back around to face Sonya. "What a tragedy. Especially for Casper, having that argument as his last memory."

"He's a mess," Sonya said with a nod.

"Do they have any idea what caused the reaction?"

"Not yet. The police processed the scene of course, bagged up everything. Apparently Kimberly had quite a few allergies, but according to Drea, no one in the family knew they were that serious."

"Wow."

Sonya slipped her feet back into her pricey shoes and pushed up from her seat. "Thank you for handling the funeral arrangements. Call me on my cell if you need anything."

"I will," I replied, rising along with her.

I walked her to the door and held it open as she passed through.

When she was a good distance away from the shop, I turned around and addressed my trio of ghostly companions. "Well, I guess now we know how she died. The next question is what the heck she's still doing hanging around in this realm."

"More importantly, how do we get her out of it?" Flapjack added.

CHAPTER 7

"On a scale of one to ten, how weird would it be for me to pack this little omelet skillet in my purse?"

I held up the small iron pan for Hayward and Flapjack to consider.

"I'd rank it a solid seven and a half," Flapjack replied.

I frowned and put the pan back on one of the stove burners. "Well, it's the smallest thing I have that's made of real iron. You know, in case Crazy Cougar and Bridezilla decide to crash my dinner plans."

Hayward's lips twitched, sending his bushy, but well-maintained, mustache into a strange dance. "My apologies, Lady Scarlet, but don't you think it might be a touch peculiar if you were to brandish a small cooking pan in the middle of a crowded dining room?"

"Agreed." Flapjack nodded. "Once it comes out of the purse, that automatically bumps it up to a full ten."

"It was worth a shot," I sagged into one of the painted chairs clustered around my small kitchen table. "Lucas will be here in a few minutes and I don't want to tell him we have a third, and potentially fourth, wheel."

"Maybe they're out somewhere in the fog, having a spooky cat-fight," Flapjack said, throwing in a few nasty-sounding yowls for effect as he slashed his front paws through the air.

I dropped my chin into the palm of my hand as I braced one elbow on the table. "Maybe."

"If you ask me, you should be dancing on the ceiling," Flapjack said. "That Kimberly woman was a royal pain in the rear. You don't have to deal with her as a client anymore and you're still getting money for the funeral flowers. It's a win-win."

"Flapjack," I said, throwing a little sternness behind the admonishment. In truth, I had to admit he had a good, albeit inappropriate, point.

"Quite the classy fellow, aren't you?" Hayward told the smug feline.

Flapjack tucked his head, his eyes glimmering with delight, and then leaped from the kitchen counter to trot back through the apartment. "I think I'll go wander around McNally's. It's their annual swordfish buffet this weekend. Might be some good smells floating around."

He started to go and I called after him, "Better hope they haven't doused it all in lemon!"

Flapjack muttered something as he vanished. Though it wasn't completely clear, after two and a half decades together, I could pretty much guess what he said. For whatever reason, despite his love of all things fish, he hated the smell of lemons. It was beyond revolting to him in ghost form—and possibly had been in life, I'd never thought to ask—and he often had his favorite sensory experiences ruined by a few sprays of the sour fruit.

Not that anyone felt sorry for him.

As soon as Flapjack was gone, I looked back at the small frying pan. "You're sure it would be weird?" I asked Hayward.

He gave a solemn nod.

"Fine." I pushed up from my chair.

"What do you think it's going to take to get rid of Kimberly?" Hayward asked, following after me as I went down the small hallway to the only bedroom in the apartment.

"Besides putting her back in her body?" I shrugged and came to a stop in front of the mirror over my dresser. I pulled my hair back and fastened it with an elastic band. "I have no idea. New ghosts are always the most difficult. They don't know what they want or need, and most of them are so angry about being dead that they can't even be helpful."

"I can still recall the moment when I first realized what had happened to me."

I shifted my eyes in the mirror to Hayward. He'd removed his top hat and was passing it back and forth, a nervous habit of his. "What did you do?"

"I woke up in the Vienna Opera House and could see my family in the crowd. I tried to go to them, to see why they were so upset, only to realize that it was me there on the ground."

"Oh, Hayward," I breathed, barely able to muster a whisper. "I'm so sorry."

In the years we'd spent together, he'd never told me the account of the moment he realized he was no longer among the living. Most awakening stories were tragic, but knowing how much Hayward adored his family made it particularly gutting.

"It took quite some time to accept the truth," he continued. He placed the hat back on his brow. "It's been so long now that it's hard to remember what it was like to be alive."

I wondered if that was a small mercy or another layer of tragedy.

"Do you think you'll ever want to move on? To the other side?"

Hayward ducked his chin and the hat concealed his face so that I couldn't read his expression. "I don't rightly know, Lady Scarlet. At one time, I thought that perhaps there was something here worth waiting for, but in light of recent events..."

He didn't need to elaborate. I realized what—or, rather *whom*—he had been waiting for.

Gwen.

Hayward had been nursing quite the crush on Gwen since our arrival in Beechwood Harbor. She made him happy and light. Even the polished crispness faded a little when she was around, almost like she was slowly revealing a new version of him, one that was ready to let go of some of his old ways and move into a new stage of life. Err, afterlife.

Sadly, all of that had come crashing to a halt and the formalities and serious tones were back.

"Just give it some time, Hayward." I didn't know what else to tell him. What Gwen had shared was in confidence. She's asked me to talk to him, but I wasn't sure how to broach the topic without saying too much. "Wait and see how things pan out. And, maybe next time, when you're interested in someone, you should tell them how you feel. Or else—"

"No matter, Lady Scarlet," Hayward interrupted. He straightened, thrusting his shoulders back. "Let's not dwell on such things. You have more than enough on your plate, I should think."

His rebuff stung but I understood the pain behind it and tried not to take offense. I turned my attention away from him and slipped on a pair of turquoise earrings and a matching necklace. I wasn't much of a jewelry fanatic; to be truthful, I wasn't a fan of any kind of accessories. I only owned two purses and less than half a dozen pairs of shoes.

My years of globe-trotting had established a habit of minimalism and even though I now had a home base and a fairly spacious closet, I hadn't changed much.

"What do you suggest I do about this whole mess?" I asked. If there was one way to perk Hayward up, it was to solicit his advice. In life, he'd been the head of a large household, responsible for all manner of problems and duties. Anytime he could revert to that role, he was a happy ghost.

He perked and I smiled at my reflection. "Truthfully, we don't know that she will continue to be a problem. Do we?"

I tilted my head. "You've got a point. I guess we don't know *what* she'll do next."

The thought was equal parts relieving and terrifying. My nerves were still frayed from dealing with my last haunt-happy harpy. It had all worked out in the end, but I wasn't in a hurry to deal with another high-maintenance ghost. And if Kimberly was anything, it was that.

~

Lucas dropped me off at my apartment following our dinner date. Stuffed, sleepy, and a little tipsy, I made my way upstairs and collapsed onto the couch.

"What's got you so goofy looking?"

I scowled as Flapjack leapt up beside me and started casually grooming himself as he not-so-silently judged me. "I am *not* goofy. Just happy. I managed a full dinner conversation without interruption, or even a hint of ghost talk."

Flapjack swiped his fluffy paw across his face. "Which, for you, is a real feat."

"Exact-ally." I giggled at my slip of the tongue.

Flapjack sighed. "You're drunk."

I shook my head. "Happy. Just happy."

"Mhmm." Flapjack eyed me and then curled into a ball

and tucked his feather duster of a tail under his chin like it was his personal pillow. Which, I supposed, it was. For some reason, the thought made me break into giggles again.

Flapjack gave a long-suffering sigh and closed his eyes.

I looked around. It was odd to only have one ghost on the premise. Despite Flapjack and Hayward's near-constant verbal sparring, it was rare to find one without the other. Additionally, Gwen had become quite the fixture in the house and shop below. "Where is everyone?"

"Hayward went out."

"Out? Out, where?"

Flapjack's brilliant blue eyes slid open and swiveled toward me. "I didn't ask. He's been extra stuffy lately."

My heart sank. "Show some compassion, Flapjack. He's having a rough time."

"Yeah, yeah. He lost his girlfriend, yada, yada."

I scowled at the sassy cat but didn't comment on his bad attitude. It wouldn't do any good anyway. "Have you seen Gwen?"

"Not since this afternoon."

"Hmm." I tapped a finger against my lips. "Oh! You know what sounds good! I have a leftover poppy seed muffin from Siren's Song." I shoved off the couch and started for the kitchen, wobbling a little.

"Didn't you *just* get back from dinner?"

"So? The muffin will help me think."

"Or at least absorb some of that booze." he muttered.

"It was two glasses of wine. Yeesh. You sound like Mom."

Flapjack made his amused sound, a cross between a purr and a sneeze. It wasn't quite the same as a laugh, but it was the closest he could manage. "We really should go visit her sometime soon. Eh, Scar?"

I frowned as I located and unwrapped the muffin. "Yeah, yeah."

My mother, Larissa, had called not two nights before to ask the same thing. When was I planning a visit home? Was I going to need to borrow money or was my inheritance still holding out? Had I met any available men?

On and on and *on*.

"You just want to go scare Fern," I replied, referring to my parent's Golden Retriever. He was still alive and well but seemed to have some kind of sixth sense when it came to Flapjack. Whenever we visited my childhood home, Fern went berserk trying to get at Flapjack's ghost. A fact that Flapjack exploited for his own amusement, teasing and torturing the poor thing from dawn to dusk.

Flapjack snorted.

I took the muffin back to the couch and flopped down beside him. He raised his head and wrinkled his nose. "Oh, oops." I covered the pastry. "I forgot it's *lemon* poppy seed."

"Mhmm. *Forgot.*"

"You have any idea how we can cheer up Hayward? I need to talk to Gwen."

"I don't know why you're so worried about it. Hayward is a grown man, not to mention he's been dead for a hundred years. I think he can take care of himself. See, this is your problem, Scar—you always poke around into other people's business and get too wrapped up."

I arched my eyebrows. "Says the cat who's followed me around like a big, fluffy shadow for over two decades."

Flapjack twitched his tail. "That's different."

"Uh huh."

Before I could lay out a defense for myself, Gwen's head poked through the front door. "Knock, knock?"

I sat up straighter and dropped the muffin into my lap. "Gwen!"

"Hello, Scarlet. Flapjack." She shimmied through the door

and floated farther into the living room. "Did you get those two ghosts sorted out?"

I shook my head. "Not exactly. But I have it under control."

"Under control?" Flapjack snorted. "You wanted to take a frying pan in your purse on a dinner date."

Gwen's eyes lit up. "With Lucas?"

"No, some Joe Schmo I met down at the market. I decided to play the field a little." I scoffed. "Of *course* it was with Lucas."

Gwen swished her hair. "It's not *that* ridiculous of a question. You know he's not the only man in town interested."

I sighed. "I don't want to know."

"I do!" Flapjack said, flashing a grin at Gwen.

Gwen swooped in and sat beside him. "Well, just yesterday, I overheard Jason Keith asking Cheryl—you know, the blonde who does dispatch—if you were seeing anyone."

"How would Cheryl know?"

"Oh, Cheryl knows everything. She's a real gossip hound," Gwen replied with a dismissive flap of her hand.

I bit down on my lower lip to keep from bursting out laughing.

Flapjack, not one to bother with self-control, snorted. "Pot. Kettle."

Gwen missed his reference and raced ahead. "We really need a day to catch up on our girl talk, because it sounds fabulous! Unfortunately, that's not what I came to tell you."

"There's nothing to catch up on. I'm seeing Lucas ... or, at least, seeing where things go with Lucas. I'm not interested in dating Jason. He's a nice guy, and he does look good in his police uniform, but he's not really my type."

"Honey, tall, dark, and handsome is *every* woman's type. Well, except maybe those women who like the surfer-boy types. Hmm. All oiled up on the beach, sand and sweat covering their chiseled bodies…"

"Gwen," I said, clearing my throat. "You're drifting."

Her eyes snapped open. "Right, right. Where was I?"

"Apparently at the start of a really cheesy boy-band music video," Flapjack replied.

Gwen held up a hand and then shook her head, as though receiving some kind of frequency from the back of her mind. "Myra! It's about M&M. She's missing."

I wrinkled my nose.

"Remember how I told you that she was having weird visions, waking up in strange places. Well, now she's gone missing. No one has seen her in two days. I have a bad feeling about it, Scarlet. We need to figure out what's going on!" Her voice ratcheted up with each word, ending somewhere between panicked and full-blown hysterical.

"Gwen. Gwen! Calm down. We'll find her." I reached over as though to pat her shoulder, but stopped short just before my hand passed through her. "I've never heard of a ghost simply *disappearing*. She's gotta be here in town, somewhere."

Gwen gulped. "I hope so."

"The next two days are going to be a little crazy now that I have to do Kimberly's last-minute funeral arrangements, but once I drop them off at the Lilac property, I'll help you find Myra. We'll call a special meeting of the support group to see if anyone else has seen her or knows where she might be."

"Okay. Thanks, Scarlet."

"Can you get everyone together? Seven o'clock?"

"Sure thing!"

A missing ghost, a posthumously alimony-hungry divorcee, and a dead bridezilla. Yup, my bingo card was officially full. Can I get a prize and go home now?

CHAPTER 8

*K*nowing how unpleasant Kimberly had been in life, I was surprised to find her funeral crowded, especially considering most of the attendees had flown in from the East Coast on such short notice. Then again, from what I'd gathered, most of the Gardner's and Schmidt's associates were the type who had private jets on speed dial.

Originally, I'd only planned to stay long enough to set up the floral arrangements, but as I was adding a few buds to the vases framing the larger-than-life portrait of Kimberly, her mother spotted me and asked me to stay through the service and reception. It was the last thing I wanted to do, but how could I say no to a grieving mother on the day of her daughter's funeral?

Guests filled the bed and breakfast, mingling together in clusters along the rows of white chairs arranged in rows throughout the large living room. The furnishings and decorations all were intended for use in weddings and other happier occasions and didn't quite reflect the somber mood of those gathered. Everyone was speaking in soft voices and occasionally glancing toward the front, at the large photo of Kimberly. Meanwhile, her mother and father clung to one another as they made the rounds, addressing friends and family.

I stayed in the back of the room, halfway in the entryway, watching the heart-wrenching scene with discomfort. I didn't belong there. I'd only known Kimberly for a few months, and I'd spent most of those wishing she was anywhere but Beechwood Harbor. Granted, I'd never gone so far as to wish for that place to be six feet under. Still, I felt like a fraud and an intruder.

"Well, well, well. Isn't this quaint?"

I jolted and whipped around to find Kimberly herself eying the procession from the foyer of the stately home.

"Seriously, what were they thinking with these flowers?"

"*That's* what you're concerned about?" I hissed at her out of the corner of my mouth. "Oh, and PS—I worked hard on those arrangements!"

Kimberly pulled a face. "Maybe it's a good thing I died before the wedding, then."

I scoffed and stalked off in the other direction. Punching a ghost on the day of her funeral wasn't the classiest move. Besides that, it would look incredibly strange to anyone that might happen to turn around and witness me karate chopping the air.

"What are you even doing here?" Kimberly asked, following after me. "It's not like we were friends or anything."

"For your information, your mother asked me to stay," I whispered.

"She probably felt sorry for you. You look all pasty and thin, like you haven't had a good meal in a while."

I ignored her and sped forward to tend to a drooping rose in one of the arrangements near the door. I was going to fix it, make one more pass through the space as the last of the guests were arriving, and then I was leaving. No one would notice one way or the other.

Kimberly followed after me like a lost dog, though for the life of me, I didn't know why. She'd made it clear she didn't care for me. I fixed the rose and fluffed a couple neighboring arrangements. Satisfied, I headed for the door, ready to leave.

"No one even looks sad," Kimberly finally said, her voice quiet and small.

I stopped walking and glanced back at her. "What? That's ridiculous. Of course they're sad!" I looked around and considered the cluster of people nearest to us. They were talking, well, more like chatting, with one another. No one was outright smiling but—

The tallest man in the group chuckled.

Heat rushed over my cheeks. "Kimberly, this is totally normal. Everyone has a different way of coping with—"

More laughter.

I cocked an eyebrow. What was going on out there?

Kimberly seemed bent on finding out for herself. She surged forward toward the group. I lunged after her, but of course there was nothing for me to snag or pull on. She was gone.

I drew in a deep breath and slid my eyes back toward the front doors. Three, maybe four feet and I'd be free. I could run for my newly-repaired delivery van and race back to the safety of my shop. I started for the door and had one hand on the handle, but something stopped me. I turned and watched Kimberly. She hovered outside the group of friends who were talking, and her face fell a little more with every passing moment. After another round of quiet laughter, she pivoted away and floated to observe a new group. Then another. And another. Each one left her more deflated.

She came to a stop in front of her parents and sister. They

were standing with Sonya, speaking in quiet, respectable tones.

"Mom! Dad!" Kimberly bellowed, inches from their faces. "Look! I'm right here!"

My chest clenched as I watched her, and my fingers slid away from the door handle.

"Please! Hear me! I'm right—" her voice broke and dissolved into sobs.

"Damn it," I cursed.

Then, something ran across my mind, a flicker of a realization. I quickly scanned the room and my jaw dropped as I put my thumb on the reason behind the sudden apprehension.

Casper, Kimberly's fiancé, wasn't in attendance.

Where was he? What could possibly keep him from her funeral? Something wasn't right. Sonya had told me there was trouble in paradise, but to skip out on the whole thing? That was cold. Ice cold.

Kimberly was sobbing at the front of the room, reduced to a silvery puddle at her parent's feet.

"Oh dear." A familiar voice sounded over my shoulder. "What's going on?"

I turned my head to look over at Gwen. Of course she would be in attendance. Weddings and funerals were always the best watering holes for gossip. She couldn't help herself. Moth to a flame. "Can you go get her? Bring her to the meeting tonight. We'll figure something out."

"Of course." Gwen floated past me and went through the throng of attendees to help pick Kimberly up from the floor. The women exchanged a few words and I headed to the exit.

I didn't *want* to deal with Kimberly, but what choice did I really have? Flapjack would mock me endlessly for being such a marshmallow, but I couldn't just leave her there, crying on the floor.

"Scarlet!"

Drat. So close.

I turned and saw Sonya hustling across the space, weaving around a crowd of people to reach me. She raised a finger when our eyes met and I released my hold on the door handle for the second time. "Is something wrong with the flowers?" I asked when she caught up to me. If her mother was anything like her daughter, then pickiness was embedded in their DNA.

"Oh, no. No. The flowers look great." Sonya cast a glance behind her. "Between you and me, no one is paying much attention to the flowers anyway. Casper's no-show has everyone talking."

"He really isn't coming?"

"No one can reach him. He's not picking up his phone and his hotel says he checked out late last night."

"Wow." I shook my head slowly. "I didn't see that coming."

"No one did."

I tilted my head. "Kimberly didn't either."

"Excuse me?" Sonya said.

Heat flushed my cheeks. "I mean, I'm sure she would have expected him be here. You know, to say goodbye."

Sonya exhaled as she gave a short nod. "I'm sure. She must be steaming in her grave!"

I glanced past her at Kimberly, clinging to Gwen like she was the last life raft in shark-infested waters. Then it hit me. She was worried that people didn't look sad enough, but hadn't said a word about Casper being MIA. Shouldn't that have bothered her more than keeping a tally of how many tissues were being used in the course of the afternoon?

"Sorry." Sonya placed her fingertips at her temples. "It's been a long six weeks. I think my brain is fried. Please don't tell anyone I said that."

I dragged my attention back to her and gave her a tight smile. "I won't."

She sighed. "This whole fiasco has me rethinking my plans to hire a partner and expand my business. Part of me wants to go back to making coffee at the local Starbucks."

"You were a barista before becoming a wedding planner?"

"That's right. Feels like a hundred years ago." She smiled slightly. "I'm good with people and I've always loved weddings. Well, at least until now. This one had everything I hate all rolled into one massive mess! I would have quit, probably half a dozen times, but to be frank, I really need the commission check. I'm trying to expand my business and can't get a loan if I don't pay off some of my existing debts. I've been putting out feelers to get a partner on board, but so far, I'm coming up empty. The commission from Kimberly and Casper's wedding will be enough to get me in the black in one fell swoop."

"Will be? You mean you're still getting it?"

Sonya nodded. "Oh, yes. They were past the point of getting a refund on any of it. I feel bad, but that's just how this business works. If you ask me, Casper and Kimberly were on the verge of implosion anyway. I don't know that they would have made it to the alter one way or the other."

I flinched at her bold statement but kept my mouth shut.

Gwen was speaking with Kimberly off to one side of a large table set up at the front of the room. There was no body present, as her parents had opted to have her sent back to their family plot in Upstate New York. Instead, two large floral arrangements flanked a huge framed picture of a younger Kimberly. I had no idea what the occasion had been, but she wore a formal dress and a ton make-up. I wondered if it was from her debutante debut.

"Speaking of, are you all set? Do I owe you a check?"

I shook my head, still trying to wrap my mind around the

jumbled thoughts. "I'm fine. It was no problem to do the flowers."

If only that were the end of my obligation.

∼

GWEN SHEPHERDED KIMBERLY into the meeting at seven o'clock, only a couple of hours after I'd last seen them at the funeral. As it turned out, Kimberly wasn't the only special guest at the emergency ghost pow-wow. Ruthie joined the crowd filling Lily Pond's retail space a few minutes after Gwen and Kimberly. The two women exchanged icy glares across the room but didn't address one another. Small mercies.

At ghost get-togethers, there was no need for snacks and cocktails, so things tended to dive right into the action, and Ruthie didn't waste a single moment. "My ex-husband has brought in a different voodoo chick," she complained, stamping her foot against the floor. "She's fairly incompetent, but did manage to get some kind of lock put in place on his bathroom door. No more messages in the mirror."

I winced. Dr. Barnes hadn't even mentioned that detail of the haunting.

"You write on his mirror?" Gwen stammered.

Ruthie flashed a conniving grin. "They're more like drawings. Atomically correct renderings of his tiny little—"

"Enough!" I barked, holding up a hand. "Ruthie, what do you want?"

I fished out the iron frying pan in case I needed back-up.

"I'm ready to make a deal," she said. "If you can get him to fork over half of the alimony, I'll leave him alone. You can even teach him the frying pan trick if that will make him feel better about me holding up my side of the bargain. He might need a little convincing to trust me."

DANIELLE GARRETT

"Gee, I wonder why," I muttered.

The bell attached to the front door jingled and I groaned. Lucas was early.

He looked up and his smile slid off his handsome face. "I'm going to assume that was an 'I'm so hungry I could eat a rubber shoe' kind of growl, not a 'this guy again?' kind of sound."

He held up a pair of white paper bags, each sporting a fair amount of grease stains. My mouth watered just imagining the fried delights they might conceal. The smell of chili-cheese fries wafted my way and I nearly drooled down the front of my t-shirt. "Though, if you need some convincing, these oughta do the trick."

"Actually, it was a 'crap, there are ten ghosts in here' kind of groan." I cast an apologetic glance around the room. It was awkward ignoring them as they stood there in a semi-circle, blinking and uneasy. Gwen was used to Lucas being around —maybe a little *too* used to him—but the others were wary of strangers and probably even more so when I blurted out their presence. "We're having a bit of a last minute meeting. There's a ghost missing."

"Missing? How does that even happen?"

"I'll explain later. Give me ten minutes?"

Lucas nodded as he rounded the front counter. He paused when he reached me and dropped a kiss to my forehead. He might look special-ops, ready to jump out of a helicopter, but inside, I was learning just how much of a romantic he was underneath the layers of sheer, rock-hard manliness. It was rapidly becoming my favorite thing about him.

"I'll take this upstairs and find a movie."

"Okay. Thanks." I watched him go with an appreciative eye, momentarily forgetting my audience. "Not *RoboCop* again!"

He laughed as he tugged open the metal security door and

started up the steep set of stairs that led to my apartment. When the door clanged shut, I turned back to face the group. "Sorry about that."

Twenty pairs of eyes blinked in unison.

"He knows about us?" one ghost in the back of the crowd asked.

"Can he see us too?" another asked, though the answer seemed obvious.

I lifted both hands, palms out to the small crowd. "Lucas knows about my gift. That's as far as his involvement goes."

I was going to make sure of it.

"Now, let's get back on track. My fries are getting cold." I sighed and swiveled my gaze to one end of the room. Ruthie, I'll speak to Dr. Barnes, but I can't make any promises. In the meantime, leave him alone, okay? I don't think turning up the temperature is going to get you anywhere. Next time, he might find himself someone who can actually get you kicked out and you'll be lucky if you just end up expelled from the house and not from the entire plane."

A collective chill went through the ghosts gathered.

Apparently, there were things worse than death.

CHAPTER 9

Ruthie departed, satisfied at least for the time being, and I attempted to bring the meeting back to order. "Now, the real reason I've called you all here is to discuss an emerging situation about Myra, or M&M, as most of us know her. Has anyone here seen her since Tuesday?"

I waited, clinging to the hope that Gwen was simply being over dramatic, but when the crowd was quiet, my heart sank.

"Wait!" Kimberly surged forward, planting herself front and center. "I thought this meeting was about me?"

My eyes slid shut. *This is what I get for trying to be nice.*

"Kimberly, we'll get to your concern in a—"

"Concern? Are you kidding me? I just came from my funeral! My *funeral*, people!"

I cocked my hip and crossed my arms. "You do realize that, excluding myself, everyone in this room has had a funeral? You can't really *pull rank* among the dead. The spirit world doesn't work like that. There is no rich or poor, important, not important, or any other classification that applies in the human world. So, while I'm happy to help, you're still dependent on my generosity and discre-

GHOSTS GONE WILD

tion, and right now, I'm more worried about the fact that a ghost who has lived here for years has suddenly up and disappeared."

Kimberly's expression soured as she mirrored my closed off posture. "Then why bother bringing me here?"

I glanced around the room and wondered the same thing. For some reason, watching her crumple and fall apart at her mother's and father's feet had awoken my compassion for the woman. Naturally, I felt compelled to help ghosts, to the point that the spirit world had eclipsed my participation in the mortal one during various seasons of life. At first, all I'd wanted to do was get Kimberly's spirit away from me and the entire town of Beechwood Harbor if possible, but that had shifted. Though the question remained: what could I really do? Her sole focus was on getting back into her body. An impossibility.

Returning my gaze to her pinched face, I drew in a slow breath and dropped my arms. "Honestly? I thought maybe being around other ghosts would prove helpful to you as you adjust to your new life."

"Life? Ha!" Kimberly surged up, moving higher and higher until her head nearly reached the ceiling. "This isn't living! All of you need to wake up!"

A wave of whispers swept through the room but no one looked angered. Instead, the faces cast up at Kimberly were filled with pity and a sad, shared understanding. I hadn't known any of the ghosts in the room long enough to have witnessed their transition. Kimberly was my first kinderghost in quite some time.

I'd forgotten how exhausting the beginning was.

"Kimberly, please try to understand," I started, raising a hand to beckon her back down. "This is your new life. You can choose to accept it and make the best of it, or you can reject it and spend years, even decades, wandering the earth growing more and more bitter with each passing day. There's only one way out and it isn't through your physical body."

Kimberly's eyes narrowed. "What is it then?"

Normally I kept talk of crossing over reserved for after a new ghost was at least a few weeks old because being dead was a lot to process without unpacking their entire history to figure out what blocked them from doing so at the time of their death. But, as in life, Kimberly was a special case and would require a different approach.

"There's another realm beyond this one. Some call it the Otherworld. The afterlife. Religious people refer to it as Heaven, eternity, etcetera."

Kimberly slowly drifted back down to the floor, like a Mylar balloon losing its last bit of helium.

"Now, I can't tell you *how* to get there, because it's different for everyone. What I can tell you is that there is probably something holding you back. Something gnawing at you. You won't find that true peace until you confront it."

"Oh ho! I already know exactly what it is," Kimberly raged, her eyes blazing again. Only this time they weren't directed at me. "This is about Casper!"

Gwen and I exchanged a troubled glance. "Your fiancé?" she ventured.

Kimberly gave a decisive nod. "We had a big fight the night that I ... died." She swallowed hard and the fire in her eyes dulled. "Maybe the universe, or whoever is in charge of this whole ghost thing, wants me to have a chance to resolve things."

"That sounds promising," I replied, adding an encouraging smile. "We can discuss that after—"

"Or, maybe I'm supposed to haunt him! Can I do that?"

"Ugh. No!"

It was going to be a long night.

The meeting came to a quick conclusion after Kimberly's eventual exit. She left in search of Casper not too long after coming up with the idea to haunt him. I probably should have tried to stop her, but it was pointless. If I'd learned anything about her during our one-sided pre-mortem collaboration, it was that she was an immovable rock. Once she made her mind up, that is.

In any case, without her theatrics and outbursts, we were able to conduct our remaining business in a timely manner. The only problem was that by the time the last ghost floated from the shop, I still had no idea where Myra was or what might have happened to her.

Gwen lingered after the other ghosts left. I tried to console her, promising that it was the beginning rather than the end of our search for Myra, but she didn't look convinced. Nevertheless, she followed me upstairs, where we found Lucas in the kitchen. He informed me that the fries were in the oven, keeping warm. I smiled as he pulled them out and tipped them onto a plate.

"Is there anything sexier than a man in the kitchen with his sleeves rolled up?" Gwen quipped, giving Lucas a look that would have made me want to claw her eyes out if she were still among the living.

Instead, I snorted and Lucas flashed a lopsided grin. "What's so funny?"

"Nothing." I smiled. "Thanks for keeping dinner warm. The meetings usually don't take that long."

"Trouble in the ghostieverse?"

"Always."

Gwen sighed. "I suppose I'll leave you two lovebirds alone."

I raised an eyebrow, pleasantly surprised that I wouldn't have to bribe her into leaving.

"I'll keep looking for Myra," she said, a troubled look crossing her permanently young face.

I gave her a nod when Lucas turned away and she waved before slipping through the living room wall.

"You want a beer? You have a killer selection in here," Lucas asked, gesturing for me to take a seat. "I can't remember the last time I met a woman with better taste in lagers than me!"

"Sexist much?" I teased.

Lucas laughed. "I'm trying to give you a compliment. Could you just roll with it for once?"

"All right, all right. Surprise me." I twisted in my seat and watched him retrieve a pair of bottles from the fridge. I had to admit, it was nice to have someone around to take care of me. I was rarely alone, what with every ghost in a ten-mile radius always on the verge of breaking and entering to ask for advice. To be honest, though, I spent way too much time in the spirit world. Besides my regular customers and vendors, I didn't know many living people in town. Holly Boldt, a powerful witch, lived across town in the Beechwood Manor with a pack of paranormal pals, and while I was familiar with all of them, we didn't spend much time together outside my frequent visits to Siren's Song, the coffee shop where she worked part time as a barista.

Lucas cracked open the bottles and sat down opposite me at the round table. "So, tell me—what are these meetings like? I was tempted to stay and watch you in action."

I smiled and reached for a fry. "You sure you haven't had your fill of ghost tales?"

"I don't think we're in any danger of that. Kind of goes with the territory now that I'm a part of your life."

His tone was a casual statement of fact, but had a

GHOSTS GONE WILD

powerful impact on me as we looked at each other across the table. After a moment, I ducked my chin and considered the sandwich on my plate. "Well then, let's see. Tonight I had Dr. Barnes's ex drop by to tell me that she was ready to strike a new deal. Apparently he tried to have her exorcised, but it didn't quite do the trick."

Lucas chuckled. "I wouldn't mind going back to Dr. Barnes's place. Maybe I could score an invite to the next Monday-night-football get-together. What do you think?"

I rolled my eyes. "I might like beer, but you'll never catch me at a football game."

He laughed a little louder and held up a hand. "Fair enough. But then I reserve the right to put it out there that I'm not getting dragged off to any kind of musical. If anything is 80 percent music and dancing, it's a no-go in my book."

"Deal." I giggled. "For a world traveler, you sure have a strong aversion to the arts. Isn't that half the fun?"

"I'd rather be climbing up a mountain or jumping off one. Now that's really art, if you ask me."

"Uncultured swine," I teased, popping another fry into my mouth.

"Oh, and the food." Lucas grinned. "That's well over half the appeal."

"What's the weirdest thing you've ever eaten while abroad?"

Without flinching, he replied, "Fire-roasted tarantulas."

"You're kidding?" I leaned back, nose wrinkled. "We are *never* kissing again. That, my good sir, is simply too far!"

Lucas roared with laughter. "I've gargled a lot of mouth wash since then, if that helps."

I shook my head. "Nope. Not even a little bit."

He reached for my hand, his eyes sparking with mischief. "We'll see about that."

Heat surged through me and I coughed to clear my throat. I might not be in danger of roasted spider remnants, but there was a good chance I was in danger of falling for Lucas Greene.

~

After dinner, Lucas took me for a quick drive to a small town a few miles up the coast. He'd visited it on his initial visit to Beechwood Harbor and wanted to take me to a small gelato shop that he swore was as close to the stuff he'd had in Rome as anything he'd had since. We ordered two overflowing cups of the decadent dessert and wandered up the coast, enjoying the sun setting over the Pacific.

"My first few months here were a little rough, at least when it came to the weather," I told him as we walked. "But I have to admit, this view is more than worth it."

He looped his free arm around my waist and I leaned into him. A few stragglers remained on the beach, but were far enough away that it felt like we had the whole thing to ourselves. The tide was going out, leaving a glittering sheen on the sand where the last rays of sunlight bounced off the water. "I've missed it too."

"Have you decided how long you're going to stay?" I asked before polishing off the last remaining bite of my creamy treat.

Lucas had purchased a one-way ticket out to Washington after he'd made a brief pit-stop at his crash-pad apartment in Los Angeles. He said he'd make up his mind once he got out here. At the time, I'd wondered if that was in order to give himself an easy out in case things fizzled between us. We'd kept in contact over the two months since his departure, but I think we both had some doubts that we'd be able to pick up where we'd left off.

Unnecessary worries, apparently, at least judging by the last few days.

"Depends," he replied in a maddeningly vague way. He took my empty gelato cup and nestled it with his own. "I know you're really busy with work this summer, what with the weddings and all that. I don't want to get in your way."

My heart sank. Was that his way of brushing me off? Was he looking for a loophole to escape through?

I folded my arms over my stomach and wished I'd thought to bring a lightweight sweater. It had reached the mid-seventies earlier in the day, but with the sun nearly gone, the temperature had dropped rapidly.

Lucas carried the trash as we wandered back up toward the small lot where he'd parked the car. The silence was overwhelming. I itched to break it, but had no idea what to say. As much as I wanted him to stay, I wasn't going to beg.

"Weddings and sorting Kimberly out," I finally said, just to say *something*. "New ghosts are always major time sucks. There's also a local ghost who has apparently gone missing. No one knows where she went."

"Sounds like you're playing some kind of ghost Whack-A-Mole," Lucas teased.

I smiled but there was a painful truth to his statement. "Welcome to my world."

We stopped at the top of the slight hill. Lucas went to deposit the trash in a receptacle while I brushed off the soles of my feet and slipped them back into my ballet flats.

"Ready to head back?" Lucas asked as he started for the car.

My heart sank a little lower but I slapped on a smile and nodded. "Sure. Thanks for the treat. You were right: just as good as the authentic stuff."

We drove back to Beechwood Harbor and Lucas dropped me off at my apartment. He followed me up, seeing me safely home as he put it, but didn't make an effort to stay.

My tortured brain replayed the conversations of the evening but couldn't figure out where things had gotten off track. In less than three hours, I'd gone from feeling like I was slipping head over heels, to wondering if maybe I'd been better off avoiding the whole dating thing completely. Eventually, I managed to shift my thoughts to Kimberly, Myra, and Ruth, but found no clarity there either. I tossed and turned all the more, until I somehow managed to fall asleep in a jumbled pile of frayed nerves, promising myself a fresh shot at all of it in the morning.

CHAPTER 10

"Scarlet? Scarlet, are you awake?"

The soothing voice pulled me from a dream-riddled sleep and I slowly came to consciousness. I opened my eyes and found Gwen hovering nearly horizontally over the top of me. I jolted and she swooped away. "Sorry!" she cried, settling on the other side of the room. "I didn't mean to scare you!"

I sat up and reached for my phone. Squinting, I tapped the screen, and the time flashed at me in bright LED lights. "Gwen, it's four in the morning. What are you even doing in my bedroom?"

I dropped the phone back onto the bedside table and rubbed my eyes to clear the blurriness.

"I know that I'm not supposed to be here, but Scarlet, something is wrong. Another ghost has gone missing!"

That brought me wide awake. "What?"

"After the meeting tonight, I made plans to catch up with … well, with Quinton," Gwen said, starting to pace back and forth. She wrung her hands and a small line had appeared between her brows. "We were supposed to meet at the park. I got there right on time and I waited, and waited. He never showed. I went to the house he haunts—you know that craftsman on Earl Lane? His roommate, Sturgeon, told me that he hadn't seen him all day!"

I sighed. "Gwen, you're getting all worked up and it could be for nothing. This is very thin, circumstantial evidence. Maybe he got busy?"

Gwen pivoted and planted her hands on her hips. Her gaze sharpened as she stared at me. "No one has seen him, Scarlet! I've gone all over town since leaving there and he's just gone! He wouldn't have just skipped out on me like that. Also, I asked Sturgeon and he said that Quinton has been having those strange dreams too, just like M&M. He never mentioned it to me, but then again, we usually end up … *distracted*. He's close with Sturgeon, so I believe him."

I held out both hands. "Okay, okay. Calm down. We'll figure this out, okay? Like I said before, ghosts can't just disappear. I mean, unless they were exorcised, but—"

"Scarlet!"

Oops.

"Gwen, please try to calm down. No one is running around exorcising stray ghosts, okay?"

"Well then where are they?" Gwen's tone was encroaching upon hysteria.

"I don't know!" I replied, a little gruffer than intended. "All I *do* know is that I'm not going to be able to do anything about it right this instant. I can't go roaming the streets at four in the morning, calling out for people who've been dead for the better part of the last decade, all right?"

Gwen looked hurt, giving a stiff lip as she nodded. "You're right, of course. I guess—I guess I panicked. It's not every day that my friends start going missing."

"Gwen, I—"

It was too late—the rest of my protest was swallowed up in a soft *pop* as she vanished from the room.

I groaned to myself and burrowed back under the covers.

∽

After Gwen's pre-dawn wake-up call, I found myself dragging through my morning routine after my alarm went off a few hours later. Luckily, it was Sunday and the shop was closed, but thanks to the last-minute funeral, I was running behind on other orders and needed to clock in a few hours of work without the distraction of phone calls and walk-in customers. But first ... coffee. I hurried to get dressed and then made my way across town to Siren's Song to join the throngs of people in search of their own morning kick-start. The line snaked around a center display filled with branded merchandise, and I shuffled into place behind a couple of older women who were discussing the outrageous price hikes at Thistle, the local market.

"Can you even *believe* what they're asking for a pound of tomatoes? Back in the old days, you could plant a full acre of tomatoes for the price of a five-pound bag!"

"Oh, I agree! It's simply outrageous! How am I supposed to make my homemade marinara with prices like that?"

By the time I reached the cash register to place my order, I was even more desperate for a coffee. A big one.

To my relief, Holly was working the opening shift and offered a bright smile as she took my order. "Coming right up."

"Thanks, Holly. You're a lifesaver. Though I'm not sure if you're saving mine or someone else's," I added, shooting a look at the two women who had apparently moved on to discussing their hairdos, if their gesturing was any indication. Wonder if the hairdresser was charging too much too?

The horror. How Gwen sat and listened to them all day was beyond me.

Holly rang me up and then relayed the order to Siren's Song's manager, Cassie Frank, who was working the espresso machine.

Within a few moments, I had my latte and a blueberry scone, and decided to take one of the few remaining tables to enjoy my breakfast treat. Knowing Gwen, she'd eventually circle back to ask for—or provide—an update on the missing-ghost situation, and I still didn't have any ideas for her.

Holly wandered through the dining room a few minutes after I sat down. She held a carafe of coffee and was offering free refills to the patrons who were getting their daily caffeine dose straight up. She stopped by my table, her carafe nearly empty. "How's business going?" she asked with a friendly smile. For a moment, I wondered which business she meant. There was my flower business, but then Holly also knew of my frequent side projects. They didn't really equate to a full-fledged business, but certainly kept me busy enough to be considered one.

"It's picked up quite a bit, actually. Especially since the Lilac B&B opened its doors."

"I'll bet!" Holly tucked a stray lock of her auburn hair behind her ear. "I was over there the other day to drop off a catering order for some conference, and saw your flowers at the front desk. Very pretty."

"Thank you." I sipped my latte. "What about you? It seems like this place is always jam-packed."

She laughed softly. "It's that time of year. The tourists come out and it feels like we don't get a spare moment for three months solid."

I glanced around the dining room. It was full, but everyone was engrossed in their own morning routines. Most people had newspapers, tablets, phones, and laptops in front of them. I decided it was safe and looked back up at Holly. "I actually had something that I wanted to ask you about."

"Fire away."

I kept my voice low. "Have you ever heard of ghosts going missing?"

"Missing how?"

"That's the problem. I'm not really sure."

I briefly caught her up, using as general terms as possible and keeping my tone soft enough that no one else could hear over the quiet hum of the ambient noise.

Unfortunately, Holly hadn't heard of a similar case. "I'm really sorry," she added. "I can ask around. If nothing else, there's always my Grandmother Honeysuckle."

"Thanks. If you hear anything, let me know. I'm sure it's nothing, or at least nothing serious, but I'd like to put Gwen's mind at ease."

Not to mention my own.

Holly nodded and said her goodbyes when Cassie called for her to cover the front. She smiled wide as she headed up to greet a second rush of morning customers filing through the doors.

As I was finishing my scone, the table beside mine cleared and the two ladies who had been in front of me in line circled the small cafe and took the table beside mine. Great. *Let the whining fest commence.*

"Do you know why there was a police car outside Matilda's bakery last night?"

An audible gasp. "You haven't heard?"

I stilled, the last bite of scone crumbling between my fingers as my ear perked. This was way better than the finer points of picking out a ripe cantaloupe.

"Penny was taken into custody for questioning."

"Whatever for?" the second woman asked. I could practically *hear* her salivating in anticipation of the juicy gossip.

"Well, I'm sure you know all about that spoiled brat from New York—the one who was getting married at that gaudy bed and breakfast?"

The other woman added a sanctimonious *mhmm* before replying, "I thought she died?"

"She did!"

"Oh."

"That's the whole point! Apparently, it was just more than an allergic reaction. The police think there was foul play."

Another gasp. Followed by some coughing. Gotta hate choking on muffin crumbs.

"They think Penny killed her? But why? Penny's a sweet girl. She couldn't so much as hurt a housefly."

The first woman sighed heavily. "There was something in the cake. That's why the police wanted to talk to Penny—it was from her shop."

"Oh my stars! I bet her mother is simply losing her mind over this."

"I'm sure! If that were my daughter, I'd be standing outside the station, banging on the doors until they let her go!"

"I wonder why they think that young woman was killed."

"I don't know, but it does seem suspicious though. You heard that her fiancé didn't even bother showing up to her funeral?"

I turned as the second woman was nodding like a bobblehead doll. "My friend Sarah's daughter works the front desk at the hotel they were staying in. She said every other night there was some kind of complaint about the noise coming from their room. And not the kind of noises you might expect to hear from the hotel suite of a soon-to-be-married couple, if you catch my drift."

I rolled my eyes; the entire population of Washington could have parasailed on *that* drift.

Some people.

"I heard they were fighting like cats and dogs. Very strange behavior, if you ask me."

"Mmhmm. Indeed."

A group of people walked between the tables on their way to the exit, briefly muffling the women's conversation.

"—real piece of work. She had Gigi reduced to tears after their trial run-through on the makeup."

"At least the wedding coordinator had good manners!"

"Well…"

"What? What did you hear?"

"I think she was looking for a way out of the whole thing," the woman clarified. "I caught her rolling her eyes after they left the Lucky Lady that day."

"Looks like she got what she wanted."

The ladies shuffled around, rising from their seats. "We should go see Matilda. Offer our support."

Code for: snoop and pry.

The two women passed by and I balled up my napkin and stuffed it into my empty coffee cup. When the front doors swung shut again, I pushed up from my table, shoved the chair in, and hurried outside. If there was even a shred of truth to the theory that Kimberly's death had been less than an accident, I had to find it; it could be the only way I'd ever get rid of her.

~

My first call was to Sonya. I barely waited until I was back at the shop before dialing her number. She didn't answer and I cursed her syrup-sweet voice as the call clicked over to voicemail.

"Good heavens!" Hayward said, appearing at my side. "Whatever is the matter, Lady Scarlet?"

I set my phone down on the counter and pushed my fingertips through my hair. "I think I might be onto something with this whole Kimberly mess. The problem is that I need to talk to Sonya and she's not answering her phone."

"Take heart. I'm sure she will get back to you soon."

I frowned at him. "You sound like her answering service."

Hayward shrugged and floated to the front window. With his back to me, he stared out the front window, watching as the small town came to life: people shuffled off to brunch or the market, cars buzzed by on their way in or out of town, and children ran in small packs, enjoying the sunshine.

"Hayward? Are you all right?" I glanced around. "Are you down here all by yourself?"

"I'm fine, Lady Scarlet. You needn't trouble yourself with a melancholy old man such as myself."

He was laying on the Oxford accent thicker than normal. Always a bad sign. It usually meant that he was homesick.

"Hayward, you're my friend," I reminded him softly. I rounded the counter and started toward him. "I'm not *troubling* myself. I'm—"

My phone rang.

"Damn." I looked between Hayward and the phone, then back again, guilt and anxiety tugging me in two directions.

"Go ahead, Lady Scarlet. I know you're frightfully busy these days."

"Hayward, don't—" I reached out but he was already shimmering on the other side of the display window. Head bent, he headed down the street, not even bothering to avoid the people hustling up and down the sidewalk.

I ground my teeth together and kicked myself for hesitating when the phone rang. Getting Kimberly sorted was an important task, but taking care of Hayward was inarguably higher up on my list of priorities.

"Hello, Sonya," I said, answering the call on the last ring.

"Hello, Scarlet. Sorry I missed your call. It's been a little ... busy."

"So I've heard. What's going on? I overheard something about a police investigation."

"That's right." Sonya paused and heaved a sigh. "I was supposed to be flying out of here this afternoon back to New York, but I've been asked to stay local until the police can speak with me. I honestly don't know much about it, but we're at the police station. Kimberly's parents and sister are in a room speaking with the detective now and I'll go in after them."

I could hear a catch in her voice, as though she were slightly out of breath. I imagined her stalking up and down the brightly lit hallways of the station.

"What have you heard? I'm desperate for information," Sonya asked.

"Just that they brought in someone from the bakery for questioning. Seems like they think there was something in her cake samples. I can't for the life of me think of the reason why."

Sonya snorted. "That's because you weren't there when we did all *three* of her tastings. The first time, she took one look at the plate of samples and stormed out!"

"Why?"

"The color of the frosting was wrong. I tried to console her, told her the samples were just for taste, not look, and that we'd figure that out later, but she refused to go back in. The second time, she took a few bites and spit it back out, insisting that she was not going to serve sugar-coated sawdust to her *very important* guests."

I cringed. The bakery was popular in several nearby

cities. I'd heard they even took orders for big events all the way in Seattle from time to time. There was no way their cake was anything *close* to sawdust. Sugar-coated or otherwise.

"I'm afraid to ask what happened on the third visit," I told Sonya, bracing for the next horrifying account.

"Yeah, you should be," Sonya scoffed. "Ironically enough, it was on the day that Kimberly passed. We'd gone in for a final shot at making it work. The venue has a similar deal with the bakery as they do with you regarding large-scale events. However, I had a feeling that if things didn't turn around, they were going to be more than happy to make an exception and let us go somewhere else. I was actually contacting bakeries in the car on the way over to the appointment." She sighed. "Anyway, at first it looked like we might have turned a corner. The colors were right, Kimberly tried the first two samples and actually seemed *pleased*, which —as you know—was a real miracle. The third sample was where it all fell apart."

"What happened?"

"There was a miscommunication. It was my fault, really. I'd heard some locals raving about their banana cake and asked Penny to slip one into the line-up, thinking maybe Kimberly would take to it. Big mistake. Kimberly spit it out, flipped over the plate of the samples, and threw a huge fit in front of a couple of other customers. Poor Penny was reduced to tears before I managed to get Kimberly out of the bakery. Drea went back to try to comfort her, to pay her for her trouble, but it didn't seem to help much. At least not according to Drea. She refused to take the money and said they weren't going to be able to fulfill the order for the wedding cake. Not that I could blame them."

"But you ended up taking samples over there later that

night, right?" I asked, recalling the conversation I'd had with Sonya at my flower shop.

"Matilda, the owner, called me that afternoon and apologized. She said they had a special custom recipe they wanted Kimberly to sample and asked if I would have her give it one more try. To be honest, I think they wanted the exposure. As you know, the wedding was going to be featured on the season premiere of *Mints on the Pillows* and all the vendors would get a mention in the credits as well as on the show's website. It would be a lot of potential revenue to walk away from. I agreed, and by some miracle, cajoled Kimberly into trying them."

"So now they think the cake was laced with something?"

"I suppose. Drea was the first one questioned since she was the one who found Kimberly. She must have told them about the whole thing and turned their suspicions to Penny."

I conjured up an image of Penny, the sweet young woman who helped her mother Matilda run the local bakery. For the most part, I got my pastry fix from Siren's Song, though a lot of their product was from the bakery, but had occasionally visited the small shop since arriving in Beechwood Harbor. She was a tall, slender woman with straw-colored hair and a shy demeanor. She reminded me slightly of Belle from Beauty & the Beast—a quiet, bookish type who preferred to spend her days lost in books and daydreams.

She was the farthest thing from a killer that I could imagine.

Then again, wasn't there some kind of phrase about the silent ones?

"Scarlet, sorry, I'm going to have to wrap this up. They're calling me back."

I started to reply, but she'd already disconnected, leaving my head spinning and my stomach churning with a dozen new questions.

CHAPTER 11

After my phone call with Sonya, the morning quickly dissolved into madness. The printer jammed while spitting out orders. An hour-long battle followed, and by the time the foul little electronic beastie was back in working order, I was running majorly behind schedule.

I trudged back into my office to take care of some paperwork. I hated that part—as my business grew, so did the amount of office work. Perhaps it was naive of me to overlook the fact that as a business owner I would be doing a whole heck of a lot more than just making pretty floral designs. There was maintenance on the shop itself, bills to pay, invoices to collect, and now, with my first official staff member, the joys of payroll were part of the mix.

Gwen swooped in as I was midway through writing a sternly worded email to the building landlord concerning an ongoing mold issue in my supply closet. "Scarlet, we need to talk!"

I groaned. "Gwen, can it wait? I'm slammed with work right now, and before you ask, *no*, I still don't have any idea what's going on. I asked Holly Boldt and she's going to do some digging. If you really can't wait, maybe try following up with her, though I doubt she's had a chance to do much yet. She's probably still at work."

I held back the urge to remind Gwen that unlike ghosts, us mortals still had other things on our minds. I couldn't drop everything and go on a wild-ghost chase when there were orders to fill and deliveries to make. Mold to annihilate.

Not to mention the icky feeling in the pit of my stomach whenever my mind wandered off and starting thinking about the strange night with Lucas.

"If you ask me, we have a bigger problem here at home," I told Gwen, unable to resist the chance to get on my soapbox. "I'm worried about Hayward. You need to talk to him."

Gwen folded her arms. "I tried. He didn't want to hear what I had to say."

"When was this?"

"This morning, before you were awake. After you *dismissed* me from your bedroom, I came down here and found him."

I ignored her passive-aggressive tone and licked my lips. "What was he doing?"

She shrugged. "I don't know. Just kind of staring into outer space."

I gave her a pointed look.

Gwen sighed. "I'll try to talk to him again. He just makes it so difficult."

"Tell me about it." I massaged my temples. "Listen, let me finish up some things here and we'll go talk to Holly and Posy, okay? In the meantime, can you please try again with Hayward? Or at least find out where he's at. It worries me when he goes off the reservation."

I couldn't explain why it bothered me. It wasn't like there

was anything that could happen to him. He was already dead. The worst had already occurred. But still ….

Gwen agreed and floated through the opposite wall that let out into the small alleyway between my shop and the one beside it.

"So, when were you going to tell me that I was murdered?"

My eyes slid closed at the seething voice over my shoulder.

So much for productivity.

"Kimberly, I don't have time for this today," I hissed when the thick metal door of the refrigerated room was closed. "As you can see, I'm in the middle of my workday. In life, you could barge in here at any given moment, ready to launch into a tirade, but those days are over. This is my world, my rules, and you have got to accept that!"

"Well, aren't you just a regular Ms. Congeniality," she sneered. "Talking to me like that on the day I find out I've been *murdered*!"

I rolled my eyes to the ceiling, silently pleading for an ounce of patience.

"Do you know how I found out? The gossiping front desk clerks at that dump of a hotel Casper and I were staying at! I was searching for him and stopped to hover over their shoulders to get a look at the registrations, and they were talking all about it."

"I'm sorry, all right? I know this isn't easy. But you have to—"

"Why would someone want to kill me?"

It took every shred of my self-control not to snort. Instead, I drew in a slow breath. "Well, to be frank with you, you weren't a very nice individual, Kimberly." I glanced over at her and found a scowl had replaced the forlorn look from moments before. "Maybe you were back in New York, but since your arrival here, you've managed to whip up quite the frenzy. The people who live and work in this town, myself included, all work very hard, and you stormed through and tore it all to little pieces with your temper tantrums and crappy attitude."

She scoffed. "Since when is having *standards* a capital offense?"

"It's not, Kimberly. I didn't say you deserved this, but you asked for motive."

"Do you think that bakery lady did it?" she asked, her tone surprisingly cool.

"Penny," I corrected and then shook my head. "And no, I don't. Penny doesn't have a mean bone in her body. I have no doubt you drove her to drink, but kill? No way."

"The concierge didn't think so either," she replied.

"Oh?"

"He thinks it was Casper." Kimberly let out a laugh. "But, of course, that's ridiculous. Casper adored me."

I considered her for a long moment but decided to keep my opinion to myself.

She met my stare but relented after a moment with a pained sigh. "Just tell me what I'm supposed to do now."

"I don't know—*ghost* things! You can go anywhere. Isn't there someplace that's more appealing than hanging around here all day?"

Somewhere? Anywhere! I wasn't going to get too picky about the details.

She didn't look convinced. "It doesn't feel *right*."

My heart sank a little. "Kimberly, listen to me, this is all brand new for you. Just like any major change, there is something of an adjustment period. Okay? Give it some time. You'll settle in."

DANIELLE GARRETT

"No. I don't think so." She shook her head. "If there's a way out, even if it's not back to my old life, I want to find it! I want to move on from all of this madness."

You and me both, sister.

I sighed. "Like I told you before, when someone dies, their body is gone but the spirit remains."

"Gee, how enlightening. I kinda figured that part out already."

My hands balled into fists. "You want me to get the iron?"

Kimberly crossed her arms. "No."

"Then drop the attitude."

She pursed her lips, but thankfully kept them closed.

"As I was saying," I continued, emphasizing each word. "Some spirits get stuck here on earth. Now, in my experience, this is usually caused by some unresolved issue leftover from their lives. So, if we figure out what has held you back, we can try to fix it."

"Then I can go?"

"It's possible. I can't really make a guarantee, but I have been doing this a long time. A long, long time ..." I paused and released a slow breath. "Anyway, if we can figure it out, you'll probably be able to cross over."

Kimberly cocked her hip. "And do you have any experience with murder victims? Seems like that would be a big, fat unresolved issue."

I cracked a smile. "I'd say this is the first time we've agreed on something."

"So, we solve the murder, I get my angel wings?"

"Something like that."

She brightened but the effect was short-lived. "How do we do that?"

I had a feeling that Kimberly wouldn't even know how to properly load a dishwasher, so asking her to try to tackle something like a potential murder investigation was a little far-fetched.

"I know one of the officers over there. He'll probably know something. I'll go talk to him after work, okay?"

"Great! I'll circle back at six so that I can go with you."

Swell. Just swell.

CHAPTER 12

As promised—or was it threatened?—Kimberly showed up at six o'clock.

And so did Lucas.

He tapped on the locked front door and my heart jumped into my throat. In the craziness of the day, I'd lost track of my anxiety over our strange post-date conversation the night before. One look at him was enough to kick it all back into high gear. I hurried to let him in, a dozen questions running through my brain. That smile, was it hesitant? Was he holding something back? Or was he happy? Was it all just a fluke?

"Hey," I said, trying to shove all the nagging thoughts to some far corner of my mind. "I wasn't expecting you."

"Yeah, I know. I called but it went to your voicemail," he said, following me inside.

"Oh, gosh. I'm sorry. It's been ridiculous around here today." I glanced at Kimberly and silently added, *and it's not over yet.*

Lucas leaned casually against the front counter. "I know

we didn't officially make plans for tonight, but I thought I'd take a chance and see if you're free."

"Who is this?" Kimberly asked, an edge of suspicion in her voice. "He can't possibly be your *boyfriend*."

"And just why not?" I snapped.

Lucas wrinkled his brow. "Sorry, are you asking ... or telling?"

"Oh! No, not you." I shot a glare at Kimberly. "Mouthy ghosts, the usual."

"Aha." His smile returned even as his brow remained slightly furrowed. "Well, if I play my cards right, maybe I can get you to agree to talk them into giving you a night off."

I eyed Kimberly, who was vigorously shaking her head.

"What did you have in mind?" I asked, flashing a sweet smile at the argumentative spirit. She sucked in her lips like she'd bitten into a lemon.

"Dinner, for starters."

I nodded. "Dinner sounds great."

Kimberly cleared her throat.

"I just have to make a quick stop. Can I meet you somewhere?"

"Sure."

We made the plans and Lucas sauntered out of the shop. I locked up after him and then returned to finish ordering some flowers on one of my favorite wholesale websites.

Kimberly watched him go. "He's really your boyfriend?"

"You know, if there's someone's love life that we should talk about, it's probably yours," I replied. "You tracked down Casper yet?"

Kimberly's gaze shifted away from me. "He went back to New York."

I frowned. "I thought the police wanted everyone to stay close until they figured out what happened to you."

"Apparently he'd already gone."

"Interesting."

Suspicious, was actually more the word I was looking for. But until I was certain where Kimberly stood with Casper, I wasn't going to voice that part of my working theory.

"Why wouldn't he have come back for the funeral?"

She licked her lips. "I don't know."

"Well, come on, if I'm going to help you, I need to know what happened. What was the fight about? The night you died?"

Kimberly looked away, her lips spread into a thin line.

"That bad, huh?"

"It was all Casper's fault," she started.

Why am I not surprised?

She scoffed, tossing her hair. "I was in the middle of explaining the seating chart to him and he wanted to talk about the budget."

"The horror," I quipped.

Kimberly shot me a nasty look but continued, unprompted. "My parents are—were—the ones paying for the whole thing, so I honestly don't know why he even cared. I mean sure, they gave me some *parameters* but those were flexible."

"Uh huh."

"Anyway, one thing led to another, and he brought up the whole house-hunting thing, and away we went!"

"What's the house-hunting thing?"

"In addition to being in the middle of planning our wedding, we're also trying to decide which house to buy. It's taken ten months of looking to even get close to something we might consider and now there are two properties. Casper leans toward one and I want the other. It's been a sore spot for a few weeks now."

My heart went out to the poor sap who'd been trying to scour the city of New York for housing that was up to Kimberly's standards. Considering her detailed preferences in the botanical world, I could only *imagine* what she would have to say about things like square footage and closet organizers. Those ten months had probably felt more like ten years.

"Okay, obviously setting wedding budgets and house hunting are two loaded topics, but how did it go from that to a screaming match so loud the front desk was getting calls about it? I also don't see how anything could have kept him from attending your funeral. I mean, that seems like a pretty big ... break."

"Oh, it was always like that between us. He'd call me selfish, I'd call him cheap."

The blasé way she said it made my eyes widen. "That didn't bother you?"

To me, that was like a big, flashing caution sign on the freeway to marriage: Turn Back! Danger Ahead!

Kimberly tilted her head. "No, not really. I mean, at the time, obviously yes. But it was normal. For us. I guess."

"So, you tossed some barbs, Casper left the hotel room. Then what?"

"I was going to take a long bath, drink some wine, and wait for him to come back." A glint sparked in her eyes. "That was always the best part. Anytime we had a blow-out fight, the making up part was always so—"

I snapped up a hand. "Stop! TMI."

Kimberly rolled her eyes.

"I get it, you were in the bath. Next?"

"Someone knocked at the door. I figured Casper was back earlier than expected and had just forgotten his key card, but it wasn't." She frowned at the memory. "It was Drea."

DANIELLE GARRETT

"With the cake samples, right?"

"Yes. Although I don't know why I was even bothering. That cake woman wasn't qualified to operate an Easy-Bake Oven!" Kimberly soured. "We were also planning to have dinner together. Drea and Casper always got along really well and he seemed to invite her to dinner every night."

A lightbulb flashed somewhere in the back of my mind. Were Casper and Drea covering something up? Something more than a friendship? It would make sense. Casper was likely at his wit's end with Kimberly's antics and turned to Drea, a sympathetic ear. Maybe one thing led to another ... it would hardly be the first time there was something scandalous going on just behind the bridal veil.

The problem was that I couldn't ask Kimberly and there was no way to find the information on my own. At least, no *good* way. I wasn't about to wander up to either Drea or Casper and ask if they'd fallen into one another's beds anytime in the last few months. Talk about an awkward conversation.

I tucked away the curl of suspicion and turned my attention back to Kimberly. "So, Drea showed up for dinner. Did you two go to dinner alone? Since Casper was gone?"

She shook her head and curled her top lip a little. "No, we argued, too."

A sigh slipped from my lips before I could throw a bridle on it.

Kimberly sank a little lower, her semi-translucent form curving into a question mark. One perk of having no bones or muscles—you could hold odd postures without fear of cramps or stiffness. "Drea told me that she agreed with Casper. Our parents were stressed about the wedding budget but hadn't brought it up to me before. I told her she was lying, that she was jealous that I was getting married and she wasn't. She told me that I was delusional and selfish. It got ugly."

"Did you two ever get along?" I asked, somehow unable to picture it. Whenever they'd been in my flower shop at the same time, the whole room would crackle with the tension. Dark looks, irritated sighs and mumblings.

Kimberly straightened. "Not really. We're five years apart. I was starting school when she was a baby. We never shared friends, or interests for that matter. Drea is ... different. She's quiet and reserved. Geeky."

"Whereas you were the captain of the cheerleading team and Homecoming Queen?" I ventured.

She didn't deny it but her lips twisted into a deep frown that left grooves at the corners of her mouth.

"What happened after Drea left?" I asked gently.

"She'd brought over some cake samples, so I got a fork and the entire bottle of wine, and went to the bath."

"What do you remember after that?"

Kimberly thought about it for a moment. "I remember that I didn't feel good. I figured it was the sugar and wine. I've been dieting like a crazy person for eight months. *Shredding for the wedding*," she added in a sing-song voice. "It all seems so pointless now."

"From what I've heard, you died from an allergic reaction," I told her. "They think it was something in the cake samples."

Her eyes didn't register any surprise. "I know. I spent most of the day at the police station."

"Oh." I rocked back onto my heels. "Well, do you think that's what happened? Does it line up?"

"I don't know. I remember getting out of the tub. I got to the phone. My throat was scratchy and my whole face itched. I thought I called the front desk, but it must not have worked or something. I'm allergic to dairy, shellfish, most type of grass, oh, and sesame seeds."

"Yikes."

She nodded. "My parents had me tested for food allergies when I was young. They thought there was a link between that and my bad grades."

My brows cinched together. "Why would they think that?"

"I had trouble concentrating in school. The teachers would call my parents and tell them I needed to see a specialist. They took me to shrinks, doctors, a nutritionist, and even some ancient guy who supposedly practiced the art of healing."

"Did any of it help?"

"Not really. But it got me out of school, so I didn't really mind." She smiled at a memory. "For a while, I convinced one of the counselors that my parents weren't letting me out of my room and would push my meals under the doors twice a day."

I blinked. "Why would you do that?"

She shrugged. "I was bored. Trying to get them to pay attention to me, I guess."

"I guess that's one way to get it."

Kimberly's expression shifted, something darkened in her eyes. "It's past six o'clock. Can't we go now? I'd really like to get this over with."

My natural curiosity made me reluctant to drop the conversation when it was clear we were right on the fringe of a breakthrough, but if she clammed up, there was nothing I could do. "Let me grab my purse."

~

Officer Jason Keith was on duty when we arrived at the

station. I asked for him at the front desk, and he appeared within minutes, wearing a bright smile. My heart sank when I realized how my impromptu visit might be misinterpreted. A couple of months back, Jason had been instrumental in helping me deal with an even more obnoxious—and ultimately, more tragic—ghost than Kimberly. It had been clear he was interested in more than a working relationship, but I was already in the beginning of my relationship with Lucas, or at the very least, emerging from the denial that I even wanted a relationship.

"Hello, Scarlet. It's been a little while," Jason said, slipping his hands into the pockets of his black police-issued slacks. He was always polished and neat, not a button or pleat out of order. I supposed it was an admirable quality, but at the same time, it was hard to imagine his attraction to me. I didn't wander around full-blown bag lady or anything, but my jeans usually bore holes at the knees, and getting dressed up meant wearing shoes that didn't have scuffs on the toes.

I returned his easy smile. "Hello, Jason. How are you?"

"Doing all right. Working a lot of overtime. The summer always brings out the crazies."

"I'll bet." I laughed, the sound hollow, and then my eyes fell on the ancient receptionist whose expression made it clear she could do without our small talk. Returning my gaze to Jason, I folded my hands together in front of me. "Listen, is there any way that I could have a few minutes? There's something I wanted to ask you about. Officially, I mean."

"Of course," Jason replied. His tone remained casual, but a flicker of something ... *disappointment* ... crossed his face. "Come on back."

He led the way, but I remembered the path from my last visit to the small station. Jason's workspace was a parceled-out patch among a cluster of desks, all separated by low partitions that didn't quite qualify them as proper cubicles. I wasn't sure why he even had a desk considering he wasn't a detective, but it seemed the force was small enough that everyone got a space to call their own. Must be some kind of morale thing, I decided as I took the seat Jason offered me.

I glanced around as I slid down into the chair. Kimberly wasn't anywhere in my line of sight. She'd followed me over, mostly keeping to herself, but was now gone.

Weird.

"What's going on?" Jason asked once he took his own seat. He sat across from me but the space was so small that our knees nearly met in the middle. "You on some new CIA mission?" he teased.

"Not this time." I crossed my legs and laced my fingers together over my knee. "Actually, it's about Kimberly Gardner. I don't know if you know, but I was hired to do the flowers for her wedding."

"Your name was on the list of potential contacts," Jason replied.

Even though I was completely innocent, the idea of my name being grouped together on some investigation notepad or dry erase board spooked me.

"Right, of course. Well, I wanted to share some information and maybe get a few questions answered too."

Jason considered me for a moment and then gave a slight nod. "Go ahead."

Being as discreet as possible, I glanced around, doing one more sweep for any sign of Kimberly. If she was helicoptering over my shoulder, the next words out of my mouth would have to be carefully chosen. As there was no sign of her, I opted to speak a little more freely. "Let me start off by saying that I'm sure Kimberly was a lovely woman and that she was simply going through a stressful time and not at her best while here in town."

Jason smiled. "Scarlet, we've talked to half a dozen

GHOSTS GONE WILD

vendors and service providers. I've got a good sense of the victim."

"Right, right."

"Did you personally have an issue with her?"

"I—uh. Well, that's kind of a funny thing. I think she was just a little ... you know?"

Jason chuckled and held up a hand, silently letting me off the hook. "Got it."

"Regardless of Kimberly's bad behavior, I think arresting Penny is way off track. Penny is one of the— "

"Arresting?" Jason interrupted, his face suddenly set in a frown. "We haven't arrested anyone. Where did you hear that? The Lucky Lady?"

"Something like that," I admitted with a scowl. I should have known that was a polluted stream.

"No one has been arrested. At this point, we're just trying to get a sense of what happened. It looks as though she suffered a severe allergic reaction and that's what eventually led to her death, but—" he paused and looked past me. "Well, this is off the record, but I think the whole thing is a little ridiculous. The department is only doing a formal investigation because of the high-profile nature of the case."

"Really?"

Jason sat back in his chair. "Was there anything else you had to say, Ms. Sanderson?"

I looked over my shoulder and saw Chief Lincoln passing through the bull pen. Aha.

"Just that I'm available if you think of anything else you need," I added in a louder than necessary voice. "Thank you for addressing my concerns, Officer Keith."

Jason snorted. "A little thick," he said out of the corner of his mouth.

"You sure?" I asked, peeking once more as Chief Lincoln exited the small space and went into what must have been his private office. "I could have added a *'thank you for protecting our community, you should get a raise!'* at the end."

He laughed and pushed to his feet. I followed. "Come on. Let me walk you out. Unless, there was something else?"

"Is it true that her fiancé went back to New York already?"

"Yeah. We've been in contact but aren't requiring him to return for questioning." He placed a hand on the small of my back and guided me back toward the short hallway that led to the front of the station. "I really wouldn't worry yourself with all this, Scarlet. It will blow over in a few days. Once the Gardners are on their way home again."

"You're probably right. It's a real tragedy though."

Jason nodded and then moved to hold open the door for me. I stepped through, lingering a moment longer. Somehow he'd managed to get me to the door without really having answered any of my questions. Then again, if he was right and it was all just a song and dance to make Kimberly's parents happy, there wasn't much to tell.

"Thanks for your time, Jason."

He nodded. "Of course. Do you uh, need a ride home? Looks like we might be getting a little rain tonight."

"Oh, thank you. I actually drove. My van's back from the shop."

He'd been the one dispatched after Lizzie rammed the bumper into a telephone pole.

"That's great!" Jason slid his hands into his pockets and beamed, but his enthusiasm looked a little forced.

"Try telling that to my credit card," I said, smiling up at him.

He chuckled and then offered a slight wave. "Have a good night, Scarlet."

"Thanks. You too, Jason."

He went back behind the door separating the offices from

the small lobby, leaving me alone with the cantankerous-looking receptionist. There still wasn't any sign of Kimberly. I smiled at the woman behind the desk but her expression remained sour.

Kimberly's sudden vanishing act had me on edge, but I couldn't go snooping through the station looking for her.

At least, not while everyone was inside. Besides, I had a dinner date.

CHAPTER 13

"You seem preoccupied."

Lucas's statement wasn't said in an accusatory way, but made my cheeks flare with heat anyway. We were barely mid-way through our entrees and while the food was delicious and the atmosphere cozy and intimate, I couldn't focus. After my visit to the police station, I'd returned home to change and found that both the shop and my apartment were ghostless. I'd gone room to room, calling out for Gwen, Hayward, even Flapjack, but got no response.

Most would probably assume that a ghost-free house would feel *less* haunted, but mine felt spookier when it was actually empty. Go figure.

I'd changed and raced off to dinner with Lucas but couldn't stop thinking about Kimberly's disappearance at the station. It didn't make sense, considering the stink she'd made about getting to tag along. Then the empty apartment …

Something was wrong.

"I'm sorry," I told Lucas, setting aside my fork.

"Are you feeling all right?"

"Yes and no."

He put aside his own fork and dropped his hands to the table, framing his dinner plate. "I think I know what this is about." He pulled in a deep breath, eyes half-closed. When he opened them again, they locked with mine and something squirmed in the bottom of my stomach. My rollercoaster of thoughts flew off the rails, sailed over Ghost Land, and crashed headlong into the Splitsville wasteland.

This was the end. He was gearing up to break things off.

My lungs tightened, refusing to draw in another breath, and as my stomach rolled again, I worried that what little of my meal I'd managed to get down was preparing to make a second appearance at the table.

I held up a finger. "Wait." I glanced around the room. The restaurant wasn't packed, but there were still far too many ears close by. If I was getting dumped, that was something I'd have to accept, but I wouldn't have him drop me like a hot potato in public. "I'm so sorry, let me just use the ladies' room."

Without waiting for him to reply, I popped up from my seat and scurried through the restaurant, nearly crashing into a waitress who was carrying a large tray of beverages. I swerved, cheeks red hot, and muttered a string of apologies before ducking into the dimly lit hallway that led to the restrooms. I placed a hand on the door to the women's restroom, took in a deep breath, and then backed up a step.

I took a sharp turn, veering off course, and pushed out the back door. The chill air bit into my throat as I broke into a run. I gulped down huge gasps of the misty air and barreled toward the corner of the lot where I'd parked my delivery van. Thank the stars we'd met at the restaurant. I threw myself behind the wheel, turned over the engine, and veered out of the spot, keeping the headlights off in case Lucas glanced out the large mirrored windows along the front of the square building.

When I hit the end of the driveway, I clicked on my blinker, fired up the headlights, and peeled out into the night.

It was a move that would put the Cowardly Lion to shame, but in that moment, flying down the highway away from heartbreak, I didn't care.

∼

THERE WERE six missed-call notifications on my phone when I finally brought myself to check. All of them were from Lucas. I sagged down onto the couch and let out a long, slow exhale. "What is wrong with me?" I asked myself.

"What did I just walk in on?"

I opened my eyes and found Flapjack staring up at me, unblinking.

He twitched his tail and then swirled it around to cover his paws. "At least you haven't started talking about yourself in the third person yet. That's when I'll start to worry."

"Gee, thanks. Your concern is always so touching, Flapjack."

He inclined his head. "So, spill. What's wrong with you?"

I leaned back and dragged my fingers through my hair, releasing the ponytail holder in the process. "Lucas was going to break up with me at dinner and rather than sit there and face it, I snuck out the emergency exit of the restaurant."

Flapjack's lips turned up at the edges. "Could have been worse," he replied. "You could have gotten yourself stuck trying to crawl out a bathroom window. Again."

I narrowed my eyes. "I *told* you that wasn't me! That was my friend."

"Sure, Scar. Your *friend*."

I picked up a pillow and chucked it at the silvery cat. The

throw pillow soared right through him of course, but I took some pleasure in striking a dead bullseye.

Flapjack, completely unconcerned, trotted across the room and vaulted up onto his favorite spot in the window. It faced the street and most days he could be found there, watching the world go by. Some things never change for a cat, living or otherwise. He glanced out the window and then turned around and faced me once again. "Why do you think he's about to kick you to the curb?"

I frowned at the harsh phrase but answered him anyway. "I just know, okay?"

"Mmm. I see. You're right. That's practically indisputable evidence."

"Since when did you turn into the Love Doctor? That's really more of Gwen's thing, isn't it?" I shot back, still scowling.

Flapjack raised one shoulder. "Maybe. But, as you may have noticed, you've scared her off. Well, either you or Hayward did. I still haven't quite decided where to lay the blame. I'm just enjoying the silence now that she's gone."

"That's mean, Flapjack."

He turned to look out the window, swishing his tail.

"You think she's really gone?" I asked after a moment. Guilt churned in my stomach. "For good?"

"I don't know for sure. All I know is that I haven't seen her since you two had your little whatever-it-was this morning. Hayward's been MIA too."

A spark of something else flared to life. Fear. M was still missing and Gwen was convinced that her new paramour was gone too. What if Gwen was right? What if Myra and Quinton weren't simply unaccounted for? What if something had actually happened to them? If someone—or something— was coming after the local ghosts, there wasn't anything stopping it from getting to my friends, either.

But what could be happening? Holly hadn't had an answer ready.

My phone buzzed again. I looked over at the screen and saw Lucas's name flash along the top. "Ugh."

"Scar, you've never been the kind to back down from a challenge before," Flapjack said, without turning back around to face me. "Why start now?"

Great. Now even the *cat* is more mature than me.

With a mumbled reply, a run-on sentence that included both "smartass feline" and "mind your own business," I grabbed the phone and answered on the last ring. "Hey, Lucas."

"Scarlet?" The relief in his voice only made me feel worse. "Is everything all right? Where are you?"

"Home?" I replied, the word sounding more like a question.

"You are?"

"I'm really sorry," I said, sighing. "I don't know what's wrong with me today."

"Today?" Flapjack scoffed.

I chucked another pillow.

"Listen, I know what you were going to say, and it's fine. Really. It is. I get that my life is a little—no, a *lot*—unconventional. On top of that, you travel nine months out of the year. We were probably kidding ourselves from the beginning that this thing could ever work out between us. So, obviously you're making the right call by ending it."

"Ending it?"

I straightened. "That's what tonight was about, right?"

Lucas barked a laugh. "No!"

My eyes went wide and swooped over to Flapjack, who had craned around to listen in. Nosy beast.

"Scarlet, I don't know what's going on with you, but that

wasn't my intention. Why would I take you out to a nice dinner just to break it off?"

"Because you're a nice guy?" I cringed, hating my lilting tone.

"I've been distracted, but it has nothing to do with you or your ... talent."

"Oh."

"Stay where you are, okay? I'll be there in ten."

"You really don't have to— "

He was already gone.

"Great!" I tossed the phone down on the couch.

"Flapjack, I think I'm losing my mind."

"Caught that." He jumped down from the windowsill and came over to join me on the couch.

"You're my oldest ..."—what do you call a ghostly cat who was part childhood pet, part long-term companion, and a giant pain in my rear?—"friend, so I trust you to tell me the truth."

"Just so long as you don't ask me if your ass looks big in that pair of jeans with the embroidered pockets."

I scowled—and made a mental note to donate said unflattering denim. "Be serious!"

"I was," he mumbled.

"Flapjack!"

"All right, all right. Calm down." He stretched, arching his back so high that his legs shook before he dropped back down into a lazy puddle. "What do you want to ask me?"

I was regretting opening my mouth, but he was the only one available. "Do you think that I ran out of the restaurant tonight because I'm afraid of having a relationship?"

"Well of course," he scoffed. "I don't have to be Gwen or Dr. Phil to see that one."

"What am I supposed to do?" I shoved up from the couch

and started pacing, my arms folded over my stomach. "This is why I don't *do* this stuff! I've never been good at it."

Flapjack cocked his head. "I don't think you're not good at it—it's like you said, you're afraid. I think you like Lucas because he's kind of unattainable. He travels, you're building something here. He'll always be at arm's length."

I spun on my heels and stared down at the pile of silvery fluff. "I'm sorry, and when was it you got your PhD in psychology? I must have missed that development."

"You leave the TV on sometimes when you leave for work. If I *happen* to end up watching daytime talk shows, it's your fault."

"I was wondering how you knew who Dr. Phil was."

He scoffed.

"I'll try to remember to switch it over to Animal Planet next time." I suppressed a smile. "But seriously, what do you think I should do?"

"Maybe it *was* better when Gwen was here," he muttered. "At least then I didn't have to run a hotline for your love-life woes."

"Oh, shut up. You love it."

He blinked slowly but couldn't conceal the sheen in his large, once-cobalt eyes. "Scar, there's nothing wrong with you. The way I see it, this is all brand-new for you. You went from growing up under a microscope to traveling the world on your own terms. Now you're starting to put down roots for the first time in your life. It's a lot of change. Adding another person, Lucas or anyone else, is another big change. As someone who's been there through it all, I'd be worried if you weren't a little off-balance."

My nose burned as tears pooled at the edges of my eyes. For all the whining I did about his near-constant presence in my life, there were a handful of moments like these that made it all worthwhile. "Thanks, fur ball."

"Anytime, Scar."

The doorbell rang and I wiped at my eyes on my way to the door. It was bad enough that I'd flown into a full-blown panic earlier in the evening; I didn't need him to think I'd been sitting alone in the dark bawling my eyes out over a pint of Ben & Jerry's finest too.

I straightened my top and ran my fingers over my hair, then pulled open the door.

Lucas stood there smiling at me, and right beside him was a pissed-off Ruthie Jasson.

"Not this again," I muttered, sending Lucas's smile crashing to the ground.

CHAPTER 14

"I'm going to go ahead and assume that I'm not here alone," Lucas said, glancing to his left and right. "Which one is it this time?"

The fact that this was suddenly so normal to him made me burst out laughing. "Ugh! I must seem completely Dr. Jekel, Mrs. Hyde!"

Ruthie crossed her arms. "I'm glad you're having a good time. Meanwhile, I barely escaped some madman wielding some kind of ghost trap!"

The laughter died on my lips with a strangled sound. "A ghost trap?" I repeated, adding a healthy dose of sarcasm.

Lucas groaned. "I'm going to put this on ice," he said, holding up a bottle of wine.

"I'm sorry, Lucas!" I said, stepping aside as he entered the apartment. Ruthie shot daggers at me but I ignored her for a moment. "Let me just—"

"It's fine. Really." He smiled and slipped past me on his way to the kitchen. "Where do you keep your wine glasses?"

"Um, will coffee cups work?"

He laughed. "Sure."

"Ruthie, you can come in, but if you're making this up, I'll personally see to your ex's wish for a full exorcism," I said, turning back to the irate ghost. If she was in full Technicolor, I had no doubt her cheeks would be the color of the wine Lucas was about to pour into a pair of mugs. I might not have another clean dish in the house, but I always kept at least a couple of coffee cups clean. Something of an unbreakable rule.

"I wouldn't be here if it weren't serious!" She sniffed. "I've recently met a man and would *much* rather be spending my evening with him than you."

"Well, well," Flapjack commented from his seat on the couch. "Who knew ghostly cougars were so in demand."

Ruthie's eyes narrowed into tiny slits as they found the patronizing feline. "Who do you think you are?" she asked, undeterred by the fact that a cat was talking, well, insulting, her.

"Ignore him," I told her, flapping a hand in his direction. "You've got five minutes. Start talking."

Ruthie glared at Flapjack for another moment and then shifted her cold stare back at me. "I don't know how he did it, but apparently Will figured out how to get rid of me for good. One minute I was standing in the kitchen, looking out at the backyard and thinking up my next move, then all of a sudden it felt like I was falling. You know as well as I do that's impossible, but that's what it felt like. The next thing I knew, I was standing in a dark room lit only by a ridiculous amount of candles. There was this man—no, a *lunatic*—staring at me. He laughed and started reciting words ... I don't know, some kind of spell, I guess."

"A spell?" Flapjack said.

Ruthie crossed her arms and glared at each of us in turn. "Is that all you two can do? Repeat everything that I say?"

"If you'd prefer, I can tell you what I'd suggest that *you* go and do." Flapjack mocked.

"That's it!" Ruthie surged up off the floor a few feet.

I held up a hand, both to silence Flapjack and to try to smooth Ruth's ruffled feathers. "Ruthie, I don't know what you expect me to do to help you. Obviously you're fine now, right?"

"What if he pulls me back again?" Ruthie replied, panic lacing her words. "There were other ghosts there, you know. They were trapped in these strange orbs. Whoever this man is, he's trapping ghosts! I barely got away!"

"What?" I hissed. "Why didn't you start with that part?"

A deep line appeared between Ruth's brows as she glared down at me. "I was doing my best, but you and your feather duster weren't making it easy!"

"Feather duster? Seriously, that's all you got?"

"Flapjack, enough!"

He scoffed but put his head down on his paws, apparently unconcerned that Ruthie might have discovered just where Myra and Quinton were being held.

"How did you get away?" I asked Ruthie.

Lucas came back into the room and offered me a mug halfway filled with a deep red wine. I took the cup from him and he went to the couch. Flapjack hissed and leaped out of the way moments before Lucas sat on—through—him.

"I screamed," she replied, as though it was a stupid question. "I don't really know how I did what happened next, but the candles all burst into flames. Big ones. The guy was caught off guard by that and turned his back. I flew right through the wall."

"Where was this? Do you think you could lead me back? We have to rescue the others."

Ruthie considered me for a moment. "I *could* ..."

"Why do I feel like there's a *but* coming?" I muttered under my breath.

Ruthie's gaze sharpened. "But—"

"There it is," Flapjack interjected.

She huffed. "But you have to do something for me first!"

I rolled my eyes. "You're kidding, right? You're seriously going to try to blackmail me?"

She didn't reply.

"Ruthie, I've tried to help you. Your ex doesn't want to listen to me and if we push him any harder, he's probably going to put out a restraining order against me!"

She shrugged. "So?"

"So? So, that would kinda be a drag," I quipped. "Yeesh, what is it with you ghosts lately? Is there some kind of disturbance in the force or something? You've all turned into self-centered rage-aholics!"

"This isn't about me, it's about my son!"

My eyes slid closed as I struggled to keep from screaming. I held up a hand. "Listen, Ruthie, I get it. And believe me, if I could help, I would. But like I said, Dr. Barnes doesn't want to negotiate and there is nothing I can do to make him come around. It's best if we both drop it. Okay?"

"What about your little ghost friends? Trapped in that dark basement. All alone. Scared," she sneered.

"You're lying."

"Oh yeah?"

"You've probably been spying around town, using whatever you can to try to force my hand into doing battle with your ex-husband, since you can't. It's not going to work, Ruthie. Now, get out!"

Ruthie scowled at me but backed up toward the door. Apparently, she didn't want to risk having me disperse her again. "I'll leave, but if you want any help from me, you'd better be prepared to offer me a better deal."

I returned her nasty glare. "Noted."

She vanished and I exhaled long and slow. "Seriously, how do I manage to get myself tangled up in this madness?"

"I prefer to look at it as a talent, babe," Lucas replied from the couch.

"That's very glass-half-full of you. I think if our positions were switched, I'd be tearing my hair out."

"Maybe if I start singing, it will scare them away. Always worked on my little brothers."

I barked out a laugh. "Really? That bad, huh?"

He hitched a shoulder. "Apparently. The year I entered the school talent show, there were a lot of earplug jokes and dive-bombing out of the garage whenever I'd start rehearsing."

I stifled a giggle with the back of my hand. "Well, as much as I'd love to hear it, we're actually alone."

Flapjack coughed.

"Minus the cat."

Lucas glanced around. "Sounded serious. What's going on?"

I sat cross-legged on the couch, my body facing him. "Lucas, can we talk about dinner first?"

He turned toward me and raised a hand to my cheek. "I'm not breaking up with you, Scarlet. Now, if you had stuck around, instead of making your very dramatic exit, you would have found that I was actually going to ask you what you thought about taking a few days off work to go have a little adventure. There are a lot of places I'd like to go while I'm out here and I'd really like for you to go with me."

"Oh."

Lucas grinned. "See? Not so scary after all."

I covered my eyes and groaned. "Gosh, I feel like such an idiot!"

He just laughed and reached for my hands, tugging them

away from my face. "You're not. Besides, it's kind of nice being the sane one in the relationship."

I eyed him. "You're not usually? That's probably something you should have told me. What are we talking here? Full straight jacket or—"

"No!" He laughed harder and pulled me against him. The warmth surrounded me and without a second thought, I nestled into his side. "I just mean that normally I'm the one wanting to go jump off cliffs, repel down mountainsides and bridges, and camp without an RV!"

"Now, that is crazy!"

"In the past, I've always been with someone who tried to hold me back or put me in a cage. In case you haven't noticed, I'm not exactly the nine-to-fiver with a mortgage and stock options."

"Drat. I was really hoping this security gig was a ruse for a really boring accounting job."

"Sorry to disappoint," he teased, smiling down at me.

"I'm glad you're not typical, or normal, or whatever the right term is. I've never felt like I belonged in that lane. But at the same time, I'm not just unconventional in a cool, wanderlust sort of way. I mean, five minutes ago, there was literally a ghost screaming about alimony payments and ghost traps like three feet away!"

"Ghost traps?"

I rolled my eyes. "She's trying to convince me that she has some super-secret information because she thinks that will get me to try negotiating with Dr. Barnes again."

"Oh." Lucas frowned. "What does that have to do with a trap? Is that even a real thing?"

I nodded and then it hit me.

"What's wrong?" Lucas asked as I jolted out of his arms, my spine ramrod straight.

"How would she know what a ghost trap is? She hasn't

DANIELLE GARRETT

been a ghost that long and from what I can see, she's spent most of it making her ex's life hell." I pushed off the couch and paced the floor, tapping a finger against my lips. "If the vision was real, the ghost trap was real, then that means she wasn't lying."

I stopped and whipped around to face Flapjack. "We have to go!"

He held up a hand. "Okay, hold on now. What *exactly* did she say?"

I filled him in on the details as I scurried around the apartment and gathered up a makeshift ghost hunting kit. Well, more accurately, a ghost-hunter hunting kit. With each item that I shoved into my duffel bag, I added a new part of the plan that was formulating in my mind.

"Okay, so there are ghosts missing, and this guy is keeping them locked up? But how is that even possible?"

"Ghosts aren't wholly invincible," I told him, pausing to pull a hoodie on. When I popped my head through, I continued. "There are things that interfere with them or the plane they live on."

"Like the iron trick?"

"Iron. Certain scents. Salt."

"So this guy could be calling up the ghosts, like with a séance? And then keeping them trapped?"

"It's possible." I stopped, ice flooding into my veins. "Or, we could be dealing with some dark magic."

"Whoa, whoa. Did you just say *magic*?"

I crossed my arms and stared up at him. "You're totally on board with the ghost thing but magic being real weirds you out?"

Lucas thought about it and then nodded. "Yup, I think that about sums it up."

I sighed. "All right. Well, then let's just put it this way, there are *ways* something can be ... charged. I have a small pouch that works as a temporary holding place for spirits. It's hundreds of years old but still holds its power."

"Gee, it would have been nice if you'd brought that up when we were dealing with Ms. Havisham over at the Lilac property!"

I shook my head. "It wouldn't have worked on Rosie. The spirit has to be willing to enter the vessel. It's how I got Hayward over here from England. You didn't think I bought him a plane ticket or something, did you?"

Flapjack snorted. "I shudder to think of enduring a transAtlantic flight with that gas bag chattering away the entire time."

I rubbed my temples. "I'm really sorry, but I have to go deal with this. Thanks for understanding."

Truthfully, I wasn't giving him room *not* to. Luckily, he was too much of a gentleman to point that out.

"Wait—you think I'm letting you go charging after some Voodoo ghost summoner all by yourself?" Lucas asked, folding his arms. He smirked. "Babe, you've gotta know me better than that by now."

CHAPTER 15

*P*rotesting, debating, and flat-out arguing got me nowhere. Lucas followed me out to my delivery van and hopped in behind the wheel as soon as I hit the button on the keypad to unlock the doors.

"Hey!" I complained as he extended a hand, silently asking for the keys. "This is my van. I'm driving."

"Sure doesn't look that way." He flashed that half-cocked smile and wiggled his fingers. "Come on. We're burning daylight."

"You don't even know where we're going!"

"Neither do you!"

I scowled, but handed over the keys and raced around to hop in the passenger seat. Flapjack was on my heels, unwilling to miss out on the adventure.

"When Gwen was telling me about Myra's episodes, she said that Myra would wake up in weird places. An attic, then the gym at the local school. So what if this ... summoner, let's say, is calling ghosts to him and then trapping them."

"I thought you said the ghost trap has to be mutual. The ghost has to want to be trapped."

GHOSTS GONE WILD

"That's the kind I have, but who knows what other ghost whisperers use?"

"Have you ever met any?"

"Yeah. Most who claim to have some kind of power are straight-up full of it, but not all of them. Like, in the whole Dr.-Barnes fiasco, apparently after I couldn't-slash-wouldn't help him, he hired some other—"

My eyes widened as I stared out the van's windshield. "That's it! I know where to go!"

"Miss me?" Ruthie asked, floating through the side of the van. Without waiting for an answer, she settled in the cargo area, sitting cross-legged on the tarp I used to keep the floor protected from water spills.

"I believe you. Happy now?" I snapped, looking at her in the rearview mirror. Yes, I can see ghosts in mirrors. There is literally no escaping them. "Now, tell me what you know about the exorcist Dr. Barnes hired after I left. Was he the man from the vision you had?"

Ruthie's face screwed up into a pinched expression. "Maybe."

"Did he say anything to you?"

She shook her head. "He didn't get a chance. I took one look around and screamed bloody murder."

I twisted back and looked at Lucas. "You remember the way to Dr. Barnes's place?"

"You kidding? I've been dreaming about that man cave all week."

I rolled my eyes but didn't prod at him. All that mattered was getting there … fast.

∼

BY SOME MERCY, it appeared that Dr. Barnes was home when we pulled into his driveway. Lights illuminated the front of the huge house, and most of the rooms inside appeared to be lit up as well. Ruthie scoffed before getting out of the van. "He runs this place like it's some kind of museum but can't afford to pay for my son's preschool? Selfish bastard."

"Ruthie," I said, working overtime to keep my voice calm. "That's not helping. Now, as we agreed in the car, I will help you but you have to stay under control. No lashing out. No tirades. And be reasonable. All right?"

"Yeah, yeah."

Lucas killed the engine and we all piled out, Flapjack included. He refused to be replaced as my right-hand ... cat? "Scar, when you are gonna buy a place like this? We could really use some more room, you know. There are too many ghosts tripping over each other at that cardboard box you call an apartment."

I frowned at him. "First of all, you and I both know there is no *tripping*. Secondly, if you think we're ever going to live in a place this size, you might want to reconsider your daily catnip intake."

Lucas laughed and reached for me, settling his palm on my back. "You don't want a McMansion someday?"

"Not in the slightest."

He pressed a quick kiss to the side of my head. "Good. Me neither."

Startled, I looked over at him, but his attention had drifted.

Don't read into it, Scar. You already damn near scared the poor guy off once tonight.

Though on second thought, I'd been the one running away, so maybe Lucas wasn't as shakable as all that. Either way, it was a commitment-phobe meltdown moment for another evening. I had ghosts to find.

We walked up to the door, a silent little quartet, and Lucas rang the bell.

Dr. Barnes answered the door and I lunged into attack mode. "I heard you're playing with a little dark magic," I said as soon as he pulled aside the oak monstrosity.

"What are you talking about?" he demanded.

"You know, you really should have called me first. You can't just trust anyone with this kind of task. I mean, honestly, it's not like there's a Yelp review system in place for exorcists." I made a clucking sound and shook my head. "Now, Dr. Barnes, if you'll allow me, I'd like to get to the bottom of this without causing any more damage."

He took a step back and Lucas moved forward, taking it as a non-verbal welcome.

I followed as Dr. Barnes backtracked into an expansive living area off the foyer.

"How did you even know about that?" he asked, glancing around his living room with a suspicious eye, as though we might have planted secret spy cameras on our previous visit.

"Unlike this *quack* you hired, I actually know what I'm doing. Ruthie told me what you had done."

Dr. Barnes's face went pale as he looked to Lucas. He nodded.

I planted my fists on my hips. "Where did you find this so-called ghost hunter?"

"I found him online." Dr. Barnes said with a resigned look.

"The joys of the modern world," Flapjack replied. "Order takeout and exorcisms all under five minutes."

"What a time to be alive," I added. "Tell me everything that happened."

Dr. Barnes considered me, trying his best to keep his stony facade intact, but it collapsed like a cheap tent. "He ruined everything! After you left, Ruthie went crazy. I couldn't get the house warm enough, the popcorn machine went berserk again—"

"It's my one cool party trick," Ruthie interjected.

"I was desperate! I went online to some forums that talk about ... well, this kind of stuff. There was one guy who offered to come and give a consultation. A *free* one, I might add."

Flapjack snorted. "Oh good, because you know, when my spiritual livelihood is on the line, the price tag is my first consideration too. Geez."

"You really want to complain about my fees?" I asked, baffled.

"Just fix it! All of it!" Dr. Barnes bellowed, waving a hand to get us to enter the home. "I don't care what it costs me anymore. All I know is that since he left, things have been worse. Screams late at night, blasts of heat and then ice. I'm halfway considering putting this place on the market and getting out of town altogether. I don't know how much more of this I can take."

I held up a hand. "There's no reason to get hysterical, Dr. Barnes."

Lucas snorted.

Dr. Barnes frowned but kept any barbed comments to himself as he crossed his arms.

I squared off with him. "I don't want your money. All I want is the name and contact information of the person who was here."

"Fine!" Dr. Barnes fished his phone out of his pocket and scrolled through it. A few moments later, he flipped it around and displayed the screen.

Dr. Padget
Peace Again Spiritual Artistry

THE PHONE NUMBER and a PO box followed. I scowled as I typed the information into my own phone. Peace Again Spiritual Artistry? Stars above. It just *sounded* like a crock.

"Thank you," I told Dr. Barnes when I finished and returned my own phone to my pocket.

"Are you going to fix it?"

I sighed. "Yes. I'll fix it. But if you want Ruthie gone for good, I'm afraid you're going to have to come to the table and negotiate regarding the funds she wants for her son."

He cursed loudly and threw his hands up.

"Ruthie?" I said, turning to find the woman standing in the arched doorway of the kitchen. "Can you come down from your starting point?"

She heaved a dramatic sigh. "Well, he'll have to go to the *second* best preschool, but I suppose I can live with that."

I rolled my eyes but didn't bother pointing out the poor choice of phrasing. Instead, I threw my attention right back at Dr. Barnes. "She's willing to negotiate."

Negotiations quickly dissolved into a shouting match that was one-sided for Lucas and Dr. Barnes, while I got the full-volume, stereo experience from both Dr. and the former Mrs. Barnes.

I was about ready to call a time-out when a groan echoed through the house, followed by a rush of frosty air. My skin instantly prickled into goosebumps and I wrapped my arms tight around my torso. "What the hell was that?" I asked through chattering teeth.

"Yes. What the hell *was* that?" Lucas asked, frantically looking around the kitchen.

"It's Ruthie! That's what I've been trying to tell you! She's a maniac. A menace!" Dr. Barnes roared.

"Dr. Barnes, that's not—"

"Tell her she can have the full payment. I'll have my

lawyers draw up the paperwork! Just get her out of here and tell her to leave me alone!"

The problem was, Ruthie wasn't anywhere to be found.

Somehow, the arctic blast had managed to silence the feuding exes and wash Ruthie away all in one swoop.

"I'll let her know," I told Dr. Barnes before reaching for Lucas's arm. He didn't object as I dragged him back through the house and we slipped out the front door.

"What the heck is going on, Scarlet?" Lucas demanded once we were outside. "I mean, I know this is all real, but that … that was something else, wasn't it?"

"I—I don't know what that was." My limbs were still trembling. "But, I think it's time we met this Dr. Padget."

CHAPTER 16

Unfortunately, with only a PO Box and a phone number to go by, our plans were hobbled before we even got to the end of Dr. Barnes's street. Google hadn't heard of Dr. Padget or his Peace Again Spiritual Artistry Services either.

And in my experience, if Google didn't even know what you were talking about, you were really up a creek.

"He has to get his mail eventually," Lucas said, still stopped at the four-way intersection since neither of us knew where we were headed.

"So we stake out the post office 24/7?" I asked, throwing in a healthy dose of sarcasm.

Lucas frowned over at me. "*No*, but it seems to me that you have a posse of paranormal partners who could organize a lookout."

What he didn't say was something along the lines of "it's not like they have anything else to do," which obviously would have been way off base. Ghosts—at least the ones in my orbit—were always up to something. That is, when they weren't randomly disappearing.

I looked out the passenger window. Ruthie still hadn't circled back to catch up with us. Where had she gone, anyway? If I had to guess, I would have bet money that she was busy setting off Dr. Barnes's popcorn machine one last time. For posterity's sake. But what if she wasn't? It was the second time that afternoon that I'd had one go AWOL mid-conversation.

First, Kimberly at the police station. She *still* wasn't back. Now Ruthie.

Something was off.

My gaze shifted to the business card still pinched between my fingers. "Dr. Padget's stealing ghosts. Myra. Quinton. And maybe Kimberly too."

"I didn't know there was a third."

I gave a slight nod. "We were at the police station. She was there one minute, gone the next. Then there was Ruthie's disappearing act just now. What if he got to them all?"

"It doesn't make any sense," Lucas replied. "Why would he want a bunch of ghosts? It's not like he can do anything with them. Right?"

My fingers closed around the card. "I—I don't know. I wouldn't think so, but unless he just wants some kind of weird museum exhibit, there must be *some* reason."

"Are there any connections between the missing ghosts? Family? Friends?"

"No. Other than the place of death, I suppose. Myra and Quinton have been haunting Beechwood Harbor for some time now. Ruthie and Kimberly are new ghosts. Kimberly's not even from here."

"Let's start with the best-case scenario," Lucas said. He lifted a finger, prepared to list the options, but quickly realized he didn't know where to begin. He dropped his hand back to the steering wheel and glanced at me. "What exactly would that be?"

"Best case?" I sighed. "It's a series of séances gone wrong. If a séance isn't conducted properly, the ghost could, in theory, not know how to find their way back. Ghosts don't travel like humans. They aren't bound to this plane, but at the same time, they can't just continent-hop. So, say someone died here, but his or her family is across the country, like in Kimberly's case. If they were to go to New York, hire some medium, and called Kimberly forth, they might get lucky. She might hear and respond to the call. At the end, she would be released, back to where she was."

"Like a video conference call?"

I barked out a laugh. "I guess so."

"So, what you're saying is that in that scenario, if the medium, or *doctor*," he continued, adding air quotes, "were to not put her back, she'd be ... stuck in New York?"

"It's possible."

He sat back and drummed his fingers along the steering wheel. We idled at the stop sign a moment longer, each lost in thought. The neighborhood was quiet; no one was coming or going so there wasn't a rush to move on. Other than the general restlessness that was beginning to make my skin crawl, of course.

"If an inexperienced medium is the best-case, then what are we looking at worst-case?"

I'd known the question was coming. Lucas was ex-military. He was the man with a plan. Then another plan in case the first one failed. The problem was that I really didn't have an answer for him. I didn't even have the beginning whispers of a plan. Whoever—or whatever—was messing with Dr. Barnes's house was out of my league.

"I wish I knew," I finally replied. Sighing, I gestured for

him to start driving again. "The shop is closed tomorrow. I always take Monday off. That should give us some time to think and come up with a better plan. Maybe we can visit the post office and see what they can tell us about the doc. I'll also see if I can get some of the ghosts to stake out the PO Box."

"Sounds like a plan. Where to now?" Lucas asked, his fingers hesitating on the turn signal.

"Lily Pond. I'll see if Flapjack and Hayward are around."

Lucas made the turn. "Hey, isn't tonight your normal ghost meeting?"

I nodded. "Yeah, but we're skipping a week since we had that last-minute one the other night."

"Gotcha." Lucas smiled at me. "The undead sure are organized."

"Mostly thanks to Gwen. That is, if she's even still talking to me."

"Why wouldn't she be?"

"She's angry that I'm not spending more time looking for Myra, the first ghost that went missing, and then Quinton, the second, who also happens to be her new boyfriend."

Lucas looked like I'd just started speaking Swahili. "Boyfriend?"

"Beau? Sweetheart? Paramour?"

"I get the concept," he said with a wry look. "I guess I'm missing the ... well, the point."

I shrugged. "The same reason anyone gets into a relationship. Companionship, shared interests, attraction."

"Huh."

I grinned over at him. "Any of those ringing a bell? After all, you're the one who got ditched at a restaurant and still came back for more. I must have some kind of hold over you." I wiggled my fingers as though consulting a crystal ball.

Not that I'd ever tried anything like that.

Lucas chuckled and dropped a hand to rest on my knee. "Nah, I'm just here for the ghosts."

"Yeah, yeah."

～

AFTER A DISTRACTED, speculation-filled dinner, we returned to my apartment. Lucas made popcorn while I picked out a movie and queued up the DVD player. "What's our current head count?" He asked, bringing a large bowl into the living room. He grinned as he shoveled a handful into his mouth.

I glanced around. There'd been more than a few occasions when I actually *was* in the company of a ghost—or two—without realizing it. They became such a fixture in my life, that sometimes, if they were quiet (which ruled out Flapjack), they could quite literally fly under my radar. "Seems we have the place to ourselves," I told him. "Which means there will be no one to join your side in protesting when I stick this baby into the machine," I said with a laugh, holding up the DVD case for one of my favorite rom-coms.

"I can't even read it from here, but I'm guessing from the ridiculous amount of white and pink on the box that I'm in for a real treat," Lucas groused. "You don't like dresses, you own fewer pairs of shoes than me, and you have kick-ass taste in beer, but you're still clinging to the romantic comedy?"

I laughed and slid the disk into the player. "It's my one girly vice."

"Aha."

"Don't worry. I'll still watch the movies where things blow up every two-point-five seconds."

"That's a relief." Lucas gestured for me. "Come here."

The music for the opening credits blared through my

modestly sized TV and I went to the couch. Lucas pulled me into his lap and my pulse jolted into double-time.

"Now, about this no-more-kissing rule," he started, grinning as he pushed a lock of hair off my face.

"Hey, you really should have thought of that before you went off eating spiders. I mean, who does that?"

He slid his thumb over my cheek, cupping the side of my face. My breath hitched as my skin caught fire. "It's a real shame," Lucas said, his voice thick and gravely. His eyes dropped to my mouth. "Because I've been missing these lips."

"I suppose I could make an exception," I whispered.

Without another moment of hesitation, he stole a sweet kiss and the movie faded to the back of my mind.

It was perfection. Better than anything on the small screen across the room.

Until...

"Well, I'm sure glad that you're enjoying time with your boyfriend. Meanwhile, mine is missing!"

My eyes popped open and I jerked back from Lucas.

"Scarlet, are you—" He followed my eyes and groaned —*not* the good kind. "Come on, now!"

"Gwen!" I snapped. "What are you doing?"

She stood in the kitchen, thumping one foot soundlessly on the floor. "I thought you cared about us, but now I see the truth."

"Argh! You can't be serious." I surged up from Lucas's lap and knelt on the cushion beside him, facing the opposite way to better glare at my suddenly irrational friend. "Gwen, of course I care! You can't just pop in here and throw around ugly accusations like that. It's not fair and it's not even close to being true. What has gotten into you?"

Gwen was one of the sweetest souls—living or otherwise —that I'd ever met. The sudden shift in her personality was startling and frustrating.

"I'm worried sick! That's what's *gotten into me*," she fired back, crossing her arms.

I closed my eyes for a moment, forcing myself to take a minute. The last thing I wanted to do was say something I wouldn't be able to take back.

"I'm trying to figure it out, Gwen," I said, reopening my eyes. "We've spent this evening tracking down some leads, but hit a dead end."

Gwen's expression remained unchanged. "What about Hayward and Flapjack? Where are they? They could be missing!"

I sighed. "They're fine. They went to see a band playing at McNally's tonight."

She huffed. "That's where you think they are. But they could have been sucked away to the Never Never, just like Myra and poor Quinton!"

"They're fine, Gwen." I drew in another slow breath, trying to slow my racing heart. "I don't want to fight with you about this. You need to trust me."

"Well, maybe I would if you weren't more concerned with solving some make-believe problem for that horrible Kimberly woman!"

The mention of her name sparked something and I realized that I *still* hadn't seen her.

Gwen misinterpreted my silence. "That's right, I saw you at the police station with her."

"You did? Have you seen her since then?"

Gwen's eye's narrowed as her posture went even more rigid. "Are you serious? You're really more worried about her than the rest of us?"

I folded my arms. "I can't talk to you when you're like this. I think you should leave."

Lucas's eyebrows rose as he glanced up at me.

"Fine!" Gwen snapped. The lights flickered as her surge of

angry energy soared through the apartment. When they went back to full strength, Gwen was gone.

I sighed and sank back onto the couch, twisting so I was facing forward again.

Lucas tucked an arm around me. I relaxed against his rock-solid chest and listened to the steady thumping of his heartbeat. "Are you all right?" he asked.

I shrugged one shoulder. "She's just upset. I know this isn't personal. Not at the core of it."

"We'll find this Dr. Padget tomorrow and get to the bottom of this whole mess."

I nodded. "Sorry about that."

He chuckled. "Part of the package, right?"

"Unfortunately." I frowned. "I mean, talk about a mood killer."

He reached for my chin and tilted it up. With a smile, he traced a fingertip over my lips. "I think we'll find a way to get it back."

I smiled. "You really don't want to watch this movie, huh?"

Lucas laughed and then captured my lips in a kiss that took us right back where we'd left off.

CHAPTER 17

*K*imberly showed her permanently made-up face the following morning as I was shuffling into the kitchen to kick on the kettle to make some coffee. I was clearing the sleep from my eyes and walked right into her, which made for an unpleasant reunion for both of us.

I jolted awake as though she'd dumped a bucket of ice over my head. I yowled, the volume on par with Flapjack's most extreme hissing fit.

"Gawd!" Kimberly screeched. "Watch where you're going!"

I rubbed my arms and gawked at her. "You could have *said* something, ya know! I wasn't paying attention!"

"Clearly."

I growled and cut a wide berth around her, continuing on my path to the kitchen. I needed a steaming cup of coffee even more after the blast of supernatural cold. "What happened to you yesterday?"

"I don't know," she said, giving her head a slight shake. "It was weird. I was there, right behind you. I remember, because I was wondering what on earth you'd been thinking when you bought those shoes. I couldn't believe some people pay money for shoes that ugly."

I scowled at her. "Point, please?"

She dropped a look down at my feet but resisted further comment. "You went inside but when I tried to follow, it was like something blocked me. I couldn't go through the door or the wall."

"Why didn't you say something?"

"I did!"

My brows knit together. "I didn't hear you say anything."

"Well the next thing I knew, it was dark, like midnight. I screamed and cried and tried to run, but it was like I was frozen. Trapped."

I went still, suddenly even colder. "Trapped?"

"That's what I said," she sniped.

"A ghost trap."

"What are you talking about?" Kimberly asked, pressing one hand to her hip.

I raked my fingers through my bed-head hair, nervously smoothing back the frizzy and kinked strands. "Kimberly, I think there's someone who is trying to capture the ghosts that live here. I don't know why, but ghosts have been going missing for several days now. We're trying to track down the person responsible, but so far we haven't had a lot of luck."

"Why would someone want to trap a bunch of ghosts?"

I shook my head. "I have no idea."

"Great!" Kimberly threw her hands up. "First I get murdered, now some lunatic is trying to ghostnap me. What's next?"

I swallowed hard. "I don't know. But—and I can't believe that I'm saying this—I want you to stay close by today."

My phone started ringing and I huffed. Abandoning the stove, I went across the living room to retrieve it.

"What if I don't *want* to?" Kimberly asked.

I ignored her and answered the call. "Hey, Lizzie. What's going on? Is everything all right?"

"Um, yeah. I just can't get inside. I don't have a key, remember?"

"It's Monday," I said, trying to keep from sighing. Could she not keep the dates straight now?

"Oh, well I thought we were working this Monday to get the flowers done for the Murram funeral…," she let her voice trail off and I wanted to melt into a puddle on the floor.

"Oh my gosh! I'm so sorry. You're 100 percent right. I'll be there in a minute."

We clicked off the call and I raced back to my bedroom to grab a robe. I threw it over my shoulders and fiddled with the sash as I hurried downstairs into the flower shop and went around to the back door to let Lizzie inside. "I'm really sorry!" I said as she came through the door. "Thank goodness you were paying attention. We would have been in a royal pickle!"

Lizzie smiled and went to put her small purse away in a basket under the cash register. "No problem." Her smile faltered a little as she took in my strange ensemble; a tattered terry-cloth robe, leopard-print slippers (they were a gift), and dabs of zit cream applied to my chin and forehead that were hopefully preventing two little monsters from ever seeing the light of day. "Umm, I can get started on something if you need a minute."

I laughed. "That would be great. Actually," I paused and opened the cash register drawer. I plucked out a twenty and handed it over. "Would you mind running to Siren's Song? Get anything you like—it's on me."

"Are you sure?"

"Yeah, of course. Mind grabbing me a hazelnut latte and a scone? Any flavor. Oh! Except that weird cheese one. Something sweet."

She laughed and tucked the money into the pocket of her jeans. "Sure thing. I'll be back in a few."

I started for the door that led to the back stairway to my apartment. "I'll leave the back door unlocked."

Lizzie left and I scurried up the stairs, surprised that Kimberly had remained behind in the apartment. She wasn't exactly familiar with the term *boundaries*. Stepping back into the apartment, I realized why; Flapjack and Hayward were back.

"What's she doing here?" Flapjack demanded, glaring at Kimberly from across the room.

"What is your problem?" Kimberly fired back. "Why don't you go hack up a hair ball or something?"

"Oh, ouch, good one." Flapjack swished his tail and stalked to my side. "Scar, I think it's time to bust out that pathetic excuse for a frying pan and send her packing. Unless, perhaps, I could talk you into a more permanent solution."

"Not right now, Flapjack. She's going to stay close today. We have a serious problem on our hands."

"Yeah, so get used to it," Kimberly growled.

Flapjack hissed.

I cast my eyes to Hayward. "Can I ask a favor?"

"I would be honored, Lady Scarlet!" He replied, springing to attention. He gave a pert nod and quickly righted his top hat. "What do you need me to do? Say the word!"

"Can you keep tabs on these two for me today? I completely forgot, but I have to work today."

"It's Monday, Lady Scarlet. The shop is never open on Mondays."

"It's not." I started down the small hallway and stepped into my bedroom. Hayward stopped at the doorway and removed his hat. He passed it back and forth. I sighed. "You can come in, Hayward."

Flapjack didn't share Hayward's qualms and stalked in, his tail pointed at the ceiling. "I'm not hanging around with that woman all day."

"You have to," I told him. "Gwen was right. Something is going on. Ghosts are vanishing right from under our noses. I don't know where they're going, but I have a lead to someone who might know. The only problem is that I can't go find him until I get through with work. So, for the next few hours, I need all three of you to stay close."

Flapjack sat on the floor between Hayward and me. "No one else is saying it, so I'm going to."

"This oughta be good," Kimberly quipped from over Hayward's shoulder.

Flapjack glowered at her, but continued undeterred. "Myra is a really nice lady, but let's be honest, she's a little *out there*. For all we know, she wandered off on her own. As for this Quinton guy— "

Hayward bristled at the name.

"—he probably left to get away from Gwen."

"Flapjack!" I scolded. "First of all, Quinton was not trying to get away from Gwen. Second, Ruthie Jasson is possibly among the missing. And to say there is some weird paranormal stuff going on at the Barnes house would be an understatement, all right?"

The more I talked, the bigger the pit in my stomach grew.

"What is going on?" Hayward asked. "Where could they all be going?"

Flapjack shrugged one shoulder and started grooming himself. "I still think there's a reasonable explanation. There's no such thing as a ghost boogeyman. For all we know, they're off having a party without us."

"Gee, I can't imagine why someone would leave you off the guest list," Kimberly snarked.

"Enough!" I held up a hand. "I don't have time to debate

this with you all morning. I need to call Lucas and tell him about the change of plans and then get some work done. Now, Lizzie is going to be in the shop with me, so I want the three of you to play nice. No troublemaking. Hayward, I'm counting on you to keep these two civil, all right?"

"Yes, my lady."

I rolled my eyes and closed the door.

~

Lizzie was already working on an arrangement when I made my way downstairs. The vase was bursting at the seams with flowers. The result was pretty, but would carry a hefty price tag. "Your coffee is on your desk," she said when I closed the door to my stairwell.

"Thank you, Lizzie. That looks really good," I said. "What order is that for?"

"It's for one that came in last night," she replied, nodding at the printer tray. I was part of a network of shops. Someone from the East Coast could order flowers from my shop and have them delivered locally. The orders printed automatically. I didn't usually get a lot, but every little bit helped as I worked to establish myself in the region.

I blinked as she added another three roses. "You're sure it's not going to go over-budget?" I asked.

She paused and pushed the order slip over the counter. Sure enough, the final cost was well into the $200 range.

"Wow."

Lizzie snorted. "I know! He must have really screwed up, huh?"

I smiled, a smart reply on the tip of my tongue, but it faded as I realized who had placed the order: Casper Schmidt.

I flipped the paper over and my heart dropped another

inch. The recipient was listed as one Drea Gardener, still listed as a resident of the hotel they'd all been holed up in for the past several weeks as the wedding plans were finalized. Kimberly wasn't content to sit on her hands back in New York, making decisions over video calls, emails, and phone consultations. No ... she wanted—needed—to be right in the action and had managed to drag Casper and Drea and Sonya along for the majority of the ride. But why was Drea still in town? Mr. And Mrs. Gardner had already flown home. Why hadn't she gone with them?

"You can*not* leave me alone with those two all day!"

I winced as Kimberly descended from the ceiling and came into full view.

"Are they okay?" Lizzie asked.

I realized she was studying my expression and I forced a smile. "Beautiful. You're getting pretty good at this, huh?"

"I'm trying my best," she replied, taking a step back to consider the bouquet from another angle. She retrieved a large cut of ribbon and returned to her workstation to tie the shiny red fabric into an artful bow. If there was one area where she really excelled, it was in bow tying. My attempts always fell slightly short, ending up a little on the mangled side of things. With wedding season in full swing, I was willing to keep her on staff just for the use of her nimble little fingers.

"They are the most boring people, or ghosts, or whatever, that I've ever met!" Kimberly whined.

"Great job!" I exclaimed. "I'm going to get a few things from the office. Be right back."

Lizzie nodded and continued fluffing and primping the florals.

I jerked my chin, indicating for Kimberly to follow me, and then marched into my small office. I closed the door, then turned and folded my arms as she floated through the wall beside me. "You can't be down here driving me crazy all day."

"What are you going to do? Iron me? Then you'd lose track of me and you already said you don't want to do that."

I ground my teeth. "I'm starting to care less and less."

Kimberly scoffed and tossed her hair. "Fine, then if I'm officially off of house arrest, I'll go see what else is going on around town." She started to go. Calling my bluff.

"Wait!"

"Why should I? You're just going to stick me back upstairs with the stuffy one and the rude one for babysitters."

"I have deliveries to make."

"I'll go with you!"

My eyes slid toward the door, thinking of the one arrangement in particular that I did not want her to see. Or even know that it existed. If she found out Casper was sending pricey flowers to her younger sister ... well, let's just say I'm pretty sure she'd find—and subsequently unleash—some major ghost firepower. In my experience, the angrier in life, the more dangerous a ghost could become on the other side of living.

"Kimberly, please—"

A knock sounded on the door.

I shot Kimberly a *zip it* look and opened the door. "Sorry to bother you, but someone's on the phone. A Jason?"

I frowned. "Okay, I'll uh—I'll take it in here."

Lizzie nodded and pulled the door closed.

"That your boyfriend?" Kimberly asked me.

"No." I sat down at my desk. "He's the officer that's investigating your death. So shush!"

That did the trick.

I picked up the line. "Hello, Jason. What can I do for you?"

"Scarlet, I'm afraid there's been some changes in the

Gardner investigation. Would it be possible for me to stop by and ask you some questions this afternoon?"

"Of course. But, what happened?"

Jason sighed. "I was wrong when I said this investigation was a formality. It looks as though Miss Gardener was, in fact murdered."

My eyes went wide and swiveled over to Kimberly.

CHAPTER 18

"Well, what did he have to say? For all your bossy demands, you still haven't actually told me anything about what's going on," Kimberly said as soon as I hung up with Jason.

"You're right." I glanced at the closed door. Lizzie was probably fine, busy working on the arrangements for the funeral. It wasn't that I thought she would dawdle. She was eager to prove her worth and was decently talented with floral arrangements. I could trust her.

"Yesterday at the station, Jason told me that he suspected the department was putting on a show. They were going through the motions of an investigation at the insistence of your parents. But, in his opinion, there weren't any signs of foul play."

"Then why am I still here?" Kimberly demanded.

"Not all ghosts are murder victims," I replied. "I never said that was the *only* reason why some spirits are left behind. In fact, up until about five minutes ago, I would have bet money that the reason you're still here is because of how things ended with Casper."

GHOSTS GONE WILD

"But now?"

My eyes shifted to the phone. "Jason—Officer Keith—is coming by with some further questions. He says there is enough evidence to suggest this wasn't an accident or mistake."

"So, that cake woman did kill me!"

"Penny! Her name is Penny! And no, I don't think she did."

Kimberly scoffed. "Well who else touched the cake? You couldn't possibly think Drea killed me. She's the only one who touched those samples."

My eyes rounded. "No! She wasn't!"

Kimberly stilled.

"Sonya picked up the cake samples from the bakery. She was originally going to take them to you, but when she found out Drea was already heading that way, they met up."

"Why would Sonya want to kill me?"

I shot her a look. "You really have to ask?"

"Yes! I do!"

Where was Flapjack when I needed him?

"The commission from my wedding was going to finance her business expansion," Kimberly said, not waiting for me to try to stumble through an actual reply. "I overheard her on the phone one day, back in New York. I was early for an appointment and she was chattering away, her office door wide open, bragging about the massive commission."

"That might be true, but according to what she told me, she wound up still getting the commission. The wedding was close enough that everything was non-refundable."

Kimberly paused, letting it sink in, then shot up from her place at the edge of my desk. "Sonya killed me? With cake?!"

"Did she know about the allergy?"

"Of course! She was in charge of putting together the menu. She knew no shellfish, dairy, the sesame seeds. It was all on the ginormous questionnaire you have to fill out to be one of her 'superstar' clients." Kimberly surged from one end of the cramped office to the other, pacing like a caged animal.

I held up a hand. "We don't know anything for certain. We have to wait and talk to Jason. I'll tell him about your —*our*, suspicions, and let him figure it out. He's the professional here. We're just two spectators with a thin hypothesis."

Kimberly crossed her arms. "Speak for yourself! I'm way more than some bystander in all of this. I'm dead!"

"All I'm saying is that we need time to get to the truth."

"No, we don't. I know it was Sonya. It makes complete sense. You know, she was always jealous of me. Constantly asking me where my clothing was from, complimenting my shoes."

I rolled my eyes when she pivoted away from me again. "Isn't that basically describing 99 percent of the Upper East Side's female population?"

She spun, her eyes blazing. "It was *different* with Sonya. Do you know that she used to make coffee? For a living?"

She said that like it were the most absurd thing she'd ever heard of, as though she weren't talking to someone who worked in the service industry.

"What if it was an accident?"

"The cake just fell into a vat of something that would be poisonous specifically to me?"

"Or, she didn't know it would kill you. You said yourself that you didn't know that your allergies were so severe."

"So she was trying to make me sick, but not dead. Well that makes it much better, doesn't it?"

I shoved up from the desk. "I'm going back to work."

"You can't!"

"I've told you everything that I know. Now, I have things

GHOSTS GONE WILD

to do. Officer Keith will be here this afternoon. So, why don't you go back upstairs, play nice with the other ghosts, and I'll come and get you when he's here. You can eavesdrop all you want."

Unfortunately, Kimberly wasn't good at following directions. As I stalked from the office, she followed half a step behind and with Lizzie around, all I could do was swipe a hand at her as though she were some giant, talking mosquito.

"How's it going on the Murrum funeral arrangements?" I asked Lizzie.

"You should have seen the way she looked at Casper!" Kimberly babbled. "You know, I bet that's why she killed me. She thought that once I was out of the way, she'd have him all to herself!"

I stopped, wanting to point out for the dozenth time that she and Casper weren't exactly the Ken and Barbie she wanted everyone to see. Nobody had missed his absence at her funeral, but sometimes I wondered if she'd blocked that out.

Then there was the order he'd placed, not knowing that I was fully entrenched in his departed fiancé's afterlife.

I couldn't tell Kimberly about the flowers. In fact, it would be best to get them out of the shop ASAP.

"The pew bows are all done," Lizzie replied.

"Bless you," I told her with a smile. "Tell you what—how about you tackle the local deliveries. We don't want anyone waiting."

Lizzie gave me a strange look. "You want me to do the deliveries?"

The last time she'd been behind the wheel, my van ended up in the shop and was released only once I'd maxed out the company credit card to pay the deductible.

"Uh huh. Sure, why not?"

"Well, I—"

"I trust you, Lizzie."

She gave me a firm nod and went to the cooler to start pulling orders. Meanwhile, I swiped Casper's order sheet from the workbench and folded it in half.

"I wonder if I should haunt Sonya," Kimberly mused, still following me around the shop.

The cooler popped open and Lizzie came out, holding the huge bouquet set to go to Drea. Luckily, if she realized who the recipient was, she wasn't letting on. "Looks like the next two after this are going to the Lilac B & B."

A sob erupted from Kimberly's mouth before she pressed both hands across it.

"That's right," I answered Lizzie. "Normally I would do it tomorrow, but since you're going out, I'd say go ahead and load them up."

She nodded and gingerly crossed the studio space, eyeing the large arrangement to make sure she didn't crash into or trip over anything. I held my breath as she shifted the vase in order to free up a hand long enough to push open the back door. When she was gone, I ducked into the cooler to gather the accompanying arrangements.

When I crossed back to shut the cooler door, Lizzie returned.

"So? Is that what I should do? Haunt Sonya? Maybe I can learn to throw things, or mess with the lights."

I pressed my lips into a thin line and continued ignoring her.

"Why aren't you saying anything?" Kimberly prodded, following after me as I helped Lizzie get the arrangements loaded into the back of the Lily Pond van. "Hellllooo?"

I kept a placid smile in place, ignoring her pestering until Lizzie was behind the wheel, giving me a thumbs up through the driver's window. She turned on the engine and I winced as the tires hit the curb. She'd put it in drive instead of reverse. Sweat beaded on my forehead, despite the cool mid-morning breeze.

Lizzie flashed another thumbs up—a double this time—and threw the van into reverse and backed down the driveway.

"Heaven help me," I muttered, turning to go back inside.

"You done ignoring me now?" Kimberly barked.

I scowled at her. Before I could tell her *just* what I thought she should go and do, Hayward and Flapjack floated down through the ceiling. "Aha, there they are. The world's worst babysitters."

Kimberly huffed. "I'm sorry, did you just say *babysitters*?"

"She sure did, creampuff," Flapjack replied.

I looked to Hayward. If he had blood in his veins, his cheeks would have turned a nice radish purple. I was sure of it.

"I'm terribly sorry, Lady Scarlet. I was—"

"Seriously?" Kimberly rolled her eyes. "What is with that whole milady routine? Give it up! It's the twenty-first century!"

Hayward bristled, reaching up to keep his hat from toppling off his head. "Now, see here!"

"You're lucky Scarlet hasn't kicked your ghostly butt to the curb yet," Flapjack interjected.

"Enough!" I yelled above the roar. "Stop it! All of you!"

All three of them went quiet, but turned to glare at me.

"Hayward. Flapjack. Upstairs."

"Lady Scarlet, I—"

I raised a hand. "I'm not mad. I just need some space."

With a miserable nod, Hayward rose from the floor and soared up to the ceiling. The top of his hat disappeared but he stopped short when a tapping sound echoed through the space. I twisted around to look out over the front counter. "Son of a..."

Casper Schmidt was standing at the door.

CHAPTER 19

"What the *hell* is he doing here?"

I glanced at her. "Kimberly, take a deep breath for me."

"I don't breathe, remember!" She snapped, her voice soaring toward hysteric.

Casper had already seen me, there wasn't a way I could slip upstairs and ignore him. "This day just keeps getting better and better," I grumbled through a forced smile as I hurried to answer the door.

"Hello Mr. Schmidt. How can I help you?"

Casper came inside as I held open the door. "I didn't realize you were closed today. I was supposed to—"

A loud chirp stopped him mid-sentence. He reached into the breast pocket of his suit jacket and retrieved a silver phone. Without apology, he frantically tapped out a message and a *whoosh* sound followed. He glanced up. "I had a delivery going out. I assumed it would be today."

"He ordered flowers from you?" Kimberly said, floating closer to Casper. She twisted her head. "Why didn't you tell me? Who are they for?"

"Um, yes, actually." I refocused on Casper. "I'm normally not open on Mondays, but as it's the busy season, I had to make an exception. Your order went out on the van about twenty minutes ago."

He tapped another message and then looked up at me. "I got into town earlier than expected."

"Right. Well, as I said, it will be delivered shortly."

"What is going on?" Kimberly demanded. "Why are you here?" she screamed at him.

"Thank you." Casper ducked his head and went back to typing frantically on his phone. He made his way out of the shop, barely breaking eye contact with the screen.

Kimberly followed him but stopped short of the door closing. When the jingle bell went quiet, she rounded on me. "What is going on around here?"

I sighed and went to lock up, feeling Kimberly's frosty glare every step. "He ordered a bouquet of flowers for Drea."

"Drea? Why?"

I slipped the keys into the pocket of my jeans and then held out both hands. "I don't know, Kimberly. I got the order this morning. Lizzie did the arrangement and is dropping them off at Drea's hotel this morning. I didn't even realize she was still in town. From what I heard, you parents jetted home the night of your funeral."

"Drea wouldn't have gone with them. She hated traveling anywhere with our parents."

"Why?"

"She would always say they were too hoity-toity. Private jets, first class lounges."

"Sounds like a real drag," Flapjack added.

"Knowing Drea, she's hanging around here, working on her *music*," Kimberly sneered. "That's all she cares about. Even when we were planning *my* wedding, all she wanted to do was get back to New York and do some stupid show with her grungy friends."

"Sending flowers is one thing," I continued, largely ignoring Kimberly. "But flying all the way back to see her? That seems serious."

Kimberly crossed her arms. "He's not *interested* in her, if that's what you're thinking. Drea could not be further from his type."

I cut a glance at Hayward and thanked my lucky stars that she hadn't been downstairs to see the lavish arrangement. It was better for everyone if she could hang onto the idea of a small, throw-together bouquet wrapped in cellophane.

"As for why he's back, there are half a dozen reasonable explanations now that I think about it. He's a marketing expert. For all I know, he was out picking up new clients while I was planning the wedding!"

It was a paper-thin theory, but I was going to let her have it.

"Who do you think he was texting the whole time?" I asked no one in particular.

Flapjack swished his tail. "The sister-in-law."

Hayward, Kimberly, and I all pivoted toward the cat. "How do you know that?" I asked.

"He set his phone down when he reached for his wallet. I saw it right there on the screen."

"Since when can you read?"

"I've always been able to read. Cats are highly intelligent creatures, thank you very much."

I rolled my eyes. "Of course. How could we forget? Although I seem to remember that back when you were alive, you had a habit of getting your head stuck in Pringles tubes."

Kimberly snorted.

"Well, what did it say?" I pressed.

DANIELLE GARRETT

Flapjack looked at Kimberly for a moment. "He was telling her that he was in town and on his way to her hotel."

I gulped.

Kimberly bristled but made a show of tossing her hair. "I'm sure there's a reasonable explanation." She inched toward the door. "In fact, I think I'll go see what's going on."

She slipped through the glass and we all watched as she floated across the street. My heart went out to her. I had a bad feeling that she wasn't going to like what she found at the hotel.

No sooner than Kimberly left, Lucas appeared. He knocked on the front door with his elbow as both hands were wrapped around coffee cups. I smiled and rushed over to answer the door.

"Right on time," I said with a smile as I took my cup. "I just chugged the last few gulps of my first one of the day."

Lucas chuckled. "Why am I not surprised? You about done here?"

I turned and considered the mess on the workbench—bits of stems, leaves, and pieces of ribbons. "Just about." I took a sip of the creamy foam on the latte and then set the cup aside and started sweeping the trash into the large can. "Still planning on going to the post office to ask about our mysterious Dr. Padget?"

Lucas went to get a broom from the corner. "Actually, I've got a better plan."

I dumped a handful of debris into the trash and looked over at him. "You do?"

He flashed a self-satisfied smile. "That's right. I might not have *the gift*, but I still have skills."

"All right, all right, Mr. *Skillz*. What exactly did you do?"

"I called the number and set up a meeting."

"Wait, what? You actually talked to him?"

"Yep. I pretended that I had a ghost extermination—" He

paused and looked around the room, cringing. "Sorry to any, uh, ghosts present."

"None taken," Flapjack replied with a wry tone.

Hayward tipped his chin.

I rolled my fingers. "They're fine. Tell me what he said!"

Lucas swiped the broom across the floor. "We have a meeting to discuss our options. Seven o'clock tonight. He gave me the address for his office."

"You do have *the skillz*," I teased.

"I got us in the door. You're the one who's going to have to figure out how to take him down."

My lips twisted into a frown. "Right. Minor detail."

Lucas laughed. "I have faith."

The bell on the front door jangled and I groaned. "Damn, I forgot to lock it up after you."

With one swoop, I cleared the rest of the trash away and brushed my hands clean on my jeans. "Be right back," I said, leaving Lucas in the back room so I could get rid of whatever customer had wandered in.

Officer Keith was standing at the counter. He smiled as I appeared and reached up to tip the brim of his hat. He didn't have the accent, but I couldn't help wondering if he was from the South. He had all the charming mannerisms down pat. "Hello, Scarlet."

"Jason! You're earlier than I expected."

"Is this an okay time?" he asked.

"Yeah, of course. How can I help?"

Lucas joined me at the counter and the smile on Jason's face faltered. He reached over the counter. "Officer Jason Keith."

"Lucas Greene," Lucas said, accepting the handshake. When he released Jason's hand, he draped his arm around my waist.

"Wait a second," Jason said, frowning at Lucas's hand

placement for a moment. "I remember you. You were here with the TV show a few months ago."

"That's right. This trip is personal though," Lucas replied, smiling down at me.

He was clearly having way too much fun with poor Jason.

"You said you had news about Kimberly?" I prompted, eager to get the pissing match over with.

Jason straightened. "That's right."

"How do you know that she was killed?"

"The autopsy showed that she died from anaphylactic shock, triggered by her allergy to sesame seeds. The cake samples were the only thing in her stomach, so we had to assume that's where the sesame seeds were from. Which, on its own, could be considered a tragic accident. Cross-contamination isn't a capital offense. However, we had to follow the investigation through. We did indeed find sesame seeds in the filling of the cake samples we retrieved from Ms. Gardner's hotel suite. Now, we did a thorough search of the bakery where the samples were prepared, but there are no sesame seeds or presence of sesame seeds. According to Matilda and Penny, they never use them in any of their baking."

"So, someone intentionally added them to the samples?"

"It looks that way."

"Who knew about the allergy?" Lucas asked.

"Close friends, family, obviously."

"Maybe it was an accident," I suggested.

Jason looked at me. "Unfortunately, the lack of sesame seeds at the bakery rules out an accident. Someone purposefully laced the cakes with the allergen."

"That's horrible."

Jason nodded in agreement. "What I wanted to ask you was what you thought of Sonya Perez, the wedding coordinator. It's our understanding that you had interactions with her over the course of the planning."

Kimberly's voice invaded my head. *She was jealous of me. Wanted Casper. Only cared about the money.*

"Scarlet?" Jason said. "Whatever you tell me is safe—it's not going to get back to her."

"I like Sonya," I finally answered. "I know she had her … *difficulties* with Kimberly—"

Flapjack scoffed. "Who didn't?"

"According to Penny, Sonya was the one who picked up the cake samples that evening. Based on that, we asked Ms. Perez if we could search her hotel room and rental car. She obliged us and in the process, we found a jar of tahini sauce, which, I'm not sure if you know, is essentially ground-up sesame seeds. Our working theory is that she stuffed some of the sauce into the samples on her way to deliver them to Kimberly's hotel room."

"What did she say when you found it?"

Jason shook his head. "She claimed to have no knowledge as to how or why the jar was there."

"But you don't believe her?"

"To be frank, I don't know what to think. She seemed sincere to me, but the evidence is pretty damning. We're testing the jar for fingerprints."

I sighed. "I'm really sorry, Jason, but I'm not sure how much I can help. Sonya did make some questionable comments about Kimberly, mostly about how picky she was and how impossible she was to deal with, but I don't think that's motive enough to do something like this."

Jason nodded and tapped the brim of his hat again. "Well, thank you for your time. If you think of anything else, please call me."

"I will."

He left the shop after one more suspicious once-over of Lucas, and I went to lock the door behind him.

"I can't believe Sonya was the one who poisoned Kimberly," I said, returning to the back room where Lucas had resumed sweeping.

"Sounded pretty open and shut to me," he said, not looking up.

A sudden thought popped into my head, and then out of my mouth before I could stop it. "She wasn't the one who delivered the samples to Kimberly that night."

"What?"

"Drea was going to have dinner with Kimberly and Casper, at their hotel. She and Sonya met up and Drea took the cake samples to Kimberly."

Lucas paused. "You think the sister is the one who did it?"

"I don't know, but we have to find out."

CHAPTER 20

Once I returned the shop to some semblance of order, Lucas and I went down to Thistle, the local market, and showed Drea's picture to one of the regular cashiers. She recognized her but couldn't tell us what she'd purchased. Lucas told the store's owner he was doing a consultation for upgrading the system and within a few minutes had talked him into letting him take a look at his security setup. We walked out with a copy of the last months' worth of security footage and Lucas ended up getting an order for some upgraded cameras and monitoring software.

"Now that's what I call multitasking," he said with a victorious smile as we slipped back into his rental car.

We grabbed Chinese take-out for lunch and went back to my apartment to watch the footage on Lucas's laptop. The whole thing sounded really badass but in reality was slow and boring. Watching days and days of people filtering in and out of the checkout lines, even on high speed, was incredibly dull.

I blame movies for giving me a fantastical view of stakeouts.

The food was long gone and I was debating going to get some eye drops when Lucas finally lunged forward and stopped the recording. "There she is!"

I leaned in, my knees bouncing nervously, and stared at the laptop screen. "It is her. And look"—I jabbed a finger at the screen—"there's the tahini!"

The video showed Drea unpacking a basket onto the small conveyor belt. A few bags of chips, some bottles of water, a loaf of bread, and then the huge jar of tahini. She glanced around nervously as she waited for the person in line ahead of her to remove his bags and exit the lane. The cashier smiled at Drea and appeared to attempt small talk, but Drea was closed down. Shut off. She took her bags and left. Lucas paused the video and then rewound slightly, stopping the footage at the first sight of Drea.

"Check out the timestamp," Lucas said, gesturing at the corner of the screen. "The night Kimberly died."

"Two hours before," I replied.

The truth sat heavy in my stomach, weighing me down. She was her sister.

"Looks like your original theory may be right," Lucas said.

"I thought it was Sonya," I said, staring blankly at him.

"I mean the part about Casper and Drea being more than future in-laws."

"Oh." My train of thought changed gears and chugged into reverse. Was that what had happened after all? Drea and Casper commiserated, maybe over a few drinks, on a night after Kimberly had thrown them out of her room or stormed off after an epic tantrum. One thing led to another, and they ended up in some kind of forbidden romance? It had all the makings of a made-for-TV romance with Kimberly starring as the villain, at least until she ended up dead.

I winced. My investigation into her death had started as a way to help her get answers and move on. I was supposed to be helping her find peace. There was no way she was going to move on once she found out about this. She'd probably go on and haunt Drea right there in her prison cell.

My gaze drifted back to the laptop and I stared at Drea's image. At least she couldn't hear Kimberly. Listening to her big sister's berating for twenty to life would definitely qualify as cruel and unusual punishment.

"What do we do now? Turn this over to the police? It still seems pretty circumstantial."

Lucas stood and paced the length of the room, one hand resting on the back of his neck. "We could try to get footage of Drea stashing the tahini in Sonya's car. Clearly that was a frame job."

"It's a start," I agreed. "Though, you'll probably have to give another *free consultation* to land us the tapes. You sure your bottom line can take it?"

He chuckled. "I got it."

"Good." I pushed off the couch and went to the small coat closet opposite the front door. I pulled out a red jacket that was lightweight but added a layer of warmth to the tank top I'd been wearing all day at work. "Do you think we should talk to Drea? The police have already taken her statement, so maybe she'd be willing to talk to us. We could offer to help her."

"Help her do what?"

"I don't know. I'm flying by the seat of my pants here!" I pushed the closet door closed, frustrated.

"Obviously."

I pursed my lips. "It's what they always do in cop shows. Offer to help keep the bad guy from taking an even bigger fall."

"Problem is, we don't have any leverage. She doesn't have to talk to us and unless the police agree with our gut feeling, they probably won't be too concerned with this either. Like you said, it's all circumstantial."

"It was just an idea," I replied, a little sour.

Lucas flashed a half-cocked grin as he pulled open the door. "Well whatever we do, let's just try to not get into a knife fight this time."

I laughed. "I can't make any promises."

"You're bad for my health, Scarlet Sanderson."

I quirked my lips. "Says the big, bad security guard. Isn't your line supposed to be a little more *danger is my middle name?*"

"Guess I missed that lesson in badass summer camp."

I gave him a playful *thwap* on the arm and went through the door. "Come on, Bond Lite."

~

IT WASN'T hard to find Drea. She was sitting in the lobby of her hotel, scribbling into a notebook in between sips from the large glass of wine to her right. She was so engrossed in whatever she was working on that she didn't look up until Lucas slid into the seat opposite her.

"Excuse me?" Her eyes flew from Lucas to me and her expression shifted once again, her eyebrows lifting. "Oh, hello, Scarlet. What are you doing here?"

Lucas kicked out the third chair at the small table and I sat down beside him, both of us facing Drea. "There's something I need to talk to you about, Drea."

"Okay. If this is about the funeral flowers, I don't have my checkbook on me but..." She was looking back and forth between us, trying to figure out what was going on.

"No." I shook my head, wishing that was the largest of the problems on my plate. "I'm afraid not. I got a visit from one of the police officers working on the investigation into Kimberly's death."

"Oh?" Drea's eyes went wide.

I watched her face, trying to catch any slight nuance that may give her away. "Have they told you the latest development?"

She shifted in her seat, glancing around the restaurant. "Um, no. I've been in a little bit of my own world the last couple of day. Speaking of ... how did you even know to find me here?"

"Casper ordered a bouquet for you from my shop."

She rolled her eyes. "Ugh. I don't know what he was thinking with that."

Lucas and I exchanged a quick sideways glance.

I cleared my throat. "Were the two of you ..."

She waited for me to finish my question, then dawning filled her eyes. "What? God, no!" Drea shook her head and scoffed. "He was way off track. He's just another self-important, arrogant a-hole in a power suit. New York is crawling with them."

"Not to mention the part where he was engaged to your sister...," Lucas pointed out, somewhat under his breath.

Drea shifted her gaze to him. "I don't even know who you are."

"This is Lucas Greene."

She shrugged and raised her brows. "And?"

I sighed. "Drea, listen to me, there's no real easy way to bring this up, but we know what you did."

She was good. I had to give her that. She didn't even blink. "I have no idea what you're talking about."

"The police know that Kimberly was purposefully dosed with sesame seeds, one of the foods she was allergic to."

"She was my sister, I'm well aware of her *many* allergies."

"Of course," I said with a sigh. "Well they turned the

bakery inside out and tested for any chance of cross-contamination. They couldn't find anything. The sesame seeds were added to the cake samples after they left the bakery."

Drea flinched. "Are you suggesting that I know anything about that?"

"Drea, we have video footage of you buying the tahini," I said, keeping my voice soft.

Lucas nodded. "It's only a matter of time before we find proof that you stashed the jar in Sonya's car once you realized what happened. We know that you tried to set her up."

Drea crumpled. Her innocent facade fell away and she leaned forward to brace her elbows on the table.

"You killed your sister and tried to make someone else take the fall."

"I didn't mean to kill her!" Drea hissed. Her eyes searched us. Urgent and desperate, begging us to believe her. "I only wanted her to get sick. Just enough to get a break from this nightmare she'd put us all in. I wanted to go home to New York to do a performance with my band, but Kimberly wouldn't hear it."

She raked her hands through her dark hair, tugging violently at the short strands. "I don't know why she even kept me here. It wasn't like she did anything but yell at me and tell me how much I was screwing up her big day."

"Why didn't you just leave anyway?" I asked. "You're an adult. A few mouse clicks and you'd have been free to fly home."

Drea scoffed and looked up at me through her hands. "You don't get it."

"No, I don't. When is murder ever the best option?" I fired back, keeping my voice low to avoid drawing the attention of the front desk clerks across the hotel lobby.

"It wasn't a murder!" Drea insisted.

I held up a hand. "Okay, how is *food poisoning* the best option?"

"My parents wanted me to stay with Kimberly. Neither of them could be bothered to come out and rein her in. Casper couldn't keep her in check. Before we left, my dad made me a deal. He told me that if I kept Kimberly calm and under budget, he'd pay for me to take a year off school and travel with my band. There was no way that was going to happen any other way. My parents hate that I even *have* a band!"

"Why did he think Kimberly would listen to you?" I asked. "In my experiences with your sister, she didn't seem like the type to listen to anyone."

"You think?" Drea snorted and threw her hands in the air. "It was an impossible task. I should have realized it. My dad probably knew all along. I was just here to keep things from spiraling too far out of control. The last time Kimberly had free rein with a budget was her sweet-sixteen party. She went on a shopping spree that put my parents back thirty grand, just buying stupid crap for her and all her friends. My parents refused to lose face by asking her friends to return the items. They didn't want to look like they couldn't afford it. Which, to be honest, they *could*. My family is old money."

"So then why worry about it?"

Drea barked out a laugh. "Because Kimberly would have blown through half a million or more, if left unsupervised. And that bitchy consultant she hired certainly wasn't going to pump the breaks. She gets paid on commission!"

"I'm really sorry, Drea, but I think you need to get a lawyer and then go to the police and confess. Even without the video footage, the police already have their suspect list down to you and Sonya. If you try to pin this on Sonya, we'll be forced to point them to the footage. Tell me, if they dust that jar for prints, are they going to find yours?"

Drea didn't respond. After a moment, Lucas nodded. "Tell

the police what you did. If you're lucky, they won't charge you with premeditated murder."

Drea started shaking. She tugged her legs up into her chest. She looked so small, perched on the chair like a child post-tantrum. After a few moments, she shook her head. "No, I can't do that. My parents will ... they'll disown me."

"*That's* you biggest concern right now?" I spat, baffled by her oddball statement. "Drea, you're going to prison on a murder charge! You need to get a lawyer, not sit there worrying about your inheritance."

Lucas rose and reached for my hand. "Come on, Scarlet. It's in her court now. She knows what will happen if she doesn't go forward on her own terms."

We left Drea as she began to sob alone at her table.

"Next step, we take this to the station," Lucas said, holding up his phone. "Then the ball will be out of our court."

I craned around to glance back at her for a few seconds, then shook my head. "The proof is still somewhat circumstantial. If she lawyers up and turns herself in, wouldn't that be better for everyone involved?"

Lucas sighed. "Maybe so, but we have an obligation to turn this over to the police, Scarlet. We have to let them do their job now."

I nodded and he tucked an arm around my waist. Right before we walked beyond the hotel, I peeked back through the wall of glass toward the table. Drea was gone.

CHAPTER 21

Kimberly and Gwen were both waiting for us back at my apartment and neither one of them looked happy. What a surprise.

"Where have you been?" Gwen demanded as soon as we walked through the door. "I've been looking all over town for you!"

"Same here!" Kimberly snapped. "I've been stuck here listening to this hippy-dippy go on and on!"

"At least I'm not a spoiled brat who only cares about herself!" Gwen fired back, her feather earrings swaying.

Hayward and Flapjack stood nearby in the kitchen, wearing matching scowls.

Flapjack glared up at me. "Scarlet, you've got to get one or both of them out of here."

"No one is making you stay, fuzzy boots!" Kimberly snapped.

"You can't talk to him like that!" Gwen retorted.

"Ladies! Enough!"

"This again, huh? We need some kind of code word for

ghosts on the premises. Otherwise you just look like a statue."

I shot him an apologetic look. "Sorry."

He shrugged. "I'll just make some popcorn. You can fill me in later."

"Glad our problems are so entertaining to you!" Kimberly shouted at his back as he went into the kitchen. Hayward and Flapjack darted apart to let him pass.

"Kimberly, stop. Now, I want to hear from both of you but—"

"I'm going first," Gwen interrupted. "I know who has Myra and Quinton!"

Kimberly huffed and crossed her arms. "This again?"

"Since I actually *care* about people beyond what they can do for me, I've been doing some research," Gwen said, cutting a glare at Kimberly.

"All right, Gwen. You can dial back the sass. I told you last night, I've been looking into it. I even have a name. We're looking for someone called—"

"Dr. Padget," she finished.

I frowned. "Yes. Actually. How did you know that?"

"I was at the Beechwood Manor last night. Holly and Posy did some digging and found this Dr. Padget and his so-called psychic services."

In all the madness, I hadn't yet circled back to check in with Holly. "What do they know about him?"

Gwen twisted her hands together. "Apparently he has a morbid fascination with ghosts and just enough power to be a danger. Posy heard that he keeps ghosts trapped in a basement somewhere."

"Great. Now I'm *really* looking forward to tonight." I sighed.

"Tonight?"

"Lucas has arranged a meeting. You're welcome to come

along. Actually, if you can get Sturgeon to come too, that might be helpful. Another pair of hands in case things get sticky."

Sturgeon was a ghost, but had somehow mastered the use of his hands. As a former Army Sergeant, he was always a good ally to have around.

Gwen looked deflated. "I'll ask him."

"Meet here, six-thirty. We're going to get them back, Gwen."

She shot one more frosty glare at Kimberly and then vanished.

Kimberly cleared her throat. "My turn?"

"Yes, but—"

"Sonya didn't kill me."

I blinked.

"Casper did." Kimberly started pacing. "I went to the hotel and got there just in time to see Casper and Drea together. He was at the door of her hotel room, asking if she got the flowers. She told him that she refused them and had the front desk throw them away."

Not gonna lie—the florist in me died a little at the thought of that beautiful arrangement sitting in a dumpster. All I could hope was that one of the employees had rescued them from such a fate.

"Apparently it had been going on for some time," Kimberly continued. "At least that's the way Drea made it sound. Can you believe that? My own fiancé trying to hook up with my sister?"

"I'm sorry, Kimberly."

"He must have poisoned me to try to get me out of the way so he could be with Drea without being shunned for switching sisters. It all makes sense. I bet he even picked that fight with me on purpose. He knows I'm a stress eater!"

"Kimberly—"

She shook her head. "You know what? I don't even care anymore. That's all in the past now."

For the second time, she threw me off kilter. Who was this mature, balanced woman hovering before me? And more importantly, where had she been when her evil counter-personality was lecturing me on the differences between eggshell, cream, and ivory?

I drew in a slow breath. "I'm glad that you're finding peace, Kimberly, but there's one more piece to this story. Drea knew all along. She kept telling me that Casper and I weren't right for each other. I should have listened."

'Kimberly! Please, listen to me."

She stopped pacing and spun around to face me. "What is it?"

"I don't know when you left, but we went to see Drea at her hotel. We just got back."

"Casper left and Drea took that stupid notebook of hers down to the hotel lobby. I came back here. I figured she'd be lost in her own world the rest of the day. I followed Casper for a while. He went to the Lilac B & B and sat down with the owner. Seemed like some kind of business meeting." Kimberly shrugged, though her expression remained perturbed. "He's not going to get away with this. You'll help me, right? You'll tell the police it was him?"

I shook my head slowly. "Kimberly, it wasn't him. It was Drea. She's the one who put the sesame seeds into the cake samples. Via tahini dressing, to be exact."

"What?" Kimberly shook her head and sank into a chair, or as close as she could, anyway. "No. No, that can't be right. She's my sister."

"I'm really sorry, Kimberly. We talked to her and she confessed. She wasn't trying to kill you. She only wanted to make you sick. She thought that in doing so, you'd give her a break from the planning so she could get back to New York for a performance."

Kimberly looked too stunned to speak.

"We stopped off at the police station on the way back here," I continued. "They have the proof they need to bring her in for questioning. The rest will have to be sorted out by lawyers."

I glanced at Hayward and Flapjack, who were suddenly fascinated by the cracks in the floor.

"Is there anything we can do for you?" I asked her, glancing over at Lucas, who was frozen in place, popcorn bag in hand.

"No. I think I'll just go."

She slid down through the floor and was gone.

"Ugh. What a horrible, horrible day," I said, throwing myself onto the couch.

"You did the best you possibly could in such a horrid situation, Lady Scarlet."

"Thanks, Hayward. It never gets easier though."

Flapjack settled beside me. "Chin up, Scar. She'll pull through. She's a New Yorker. They're tough."

I mustered a smile and wished I could reach over and pat him on the head.

∼

SIX-THIRTY ROLLED AROUND ALL TOO SOON and I had to shove aside the mountain of sadness over Kimberly's tragic story and focus my efforts on the impending ghost-rescue mission. Right on the dot, Gwen appeared with Sturgeon, who greeted me with a salute. "Gwen informs me my assistance is needed."

"That's right. I'm sure she's brought you up to speed?"

"Yes, ma'am." He nodded. "This young man looks ready for action!"

I smiled. He was referring to Lucas, who was decked out in all black, a Taser strapped to his hip. In fact, it was the exact weapon that he'd turned on me the very first time that we'd met. Hopefully, he wouldn't need it.

I smiled and told Lucas what Sturgeon had said about him. "He's complimenting your readiness, soldier."

Lucas grinned. "Always."

"All right. Planning battles isn't really my forte, but in the spirit of preparedness, if we get separated, I want Hayward and Flapjack to stay with me. Gwen and Sturgeon, you'll be more help to Lucas."

Sturgeon saluted Lucas.

"He saluted you," I said out of the corner of my mouth.

Lucas offered a salute of his own. To a spot about four feet away from where Sturgeon stood.

It's the thought that counts, right?

I addressed the whole group. "I don't know who this Dr. Padget is, but from what we've heard, he has some supernatural power. We'll just have to figure out how much. We're not going in ... uh, Taser's blaring, but—"

"*Blazing*," Flapjack and Lucas corrected.

"Whatever." I rolled my eyes. "The point is that I want to keep this as peaceful as possible. Let's also go in with the assumption that he can see and hear you guys, so please," I swiveled my gaze to Flapjack, "let's keep our snarky commentary to a minimum. All right?"

Flapjack looked up at Hayward. "Why's she looking at me?"

Hayward sighed. "Let's go."

"Now, back to your regularly scheduled ghost-busting programming," Lucas teased as we pulled into the parking lot of a small apartment.

I glanced at him out of the corner of my eye. He wore a smile, but his eyes were all business. Dark and deadly.

Yeesh, I'm glad I didn't have to meet him in a dark alley. Then again, that was very nearly how we'd met.

"As long as he agrees to let Myra and Quinton go free, we don't have to have a war," I reminded him.

"Fine with me. War wasn't on my mind for this trip, anyway. I was planning on being a lover, not a fighter." He kissed me before I could object to the sheer cheesiness.

"Get a room!" Flapjack protested from the floorboards.

"No kidding," Gwen added, and it's a good thing I was already sitting or I would have fallen over. She lived for sappy moments like that.

"Man, that's when you know Gwen is pissed," Flapjack said, jumping out of the car. I pushed open my door and heard him say, "She didn't need a swooning couch for a line like that."

"We're not here to discuss Scarlett's love life," Gwen admonished him. "There will be plenty of time for that after we rescue Myra and Quinton."

I sighed. "Which apartment is it?" I asked as we started up toward the building.

Lucas jerked his chin at the first building in the small cluster. "17A."

"Why is he working out of an apartment?"

"I don't know. I didn't play twenty questions with the guy over the phone, all right?" Lucas replied. "Just follow my lead. As far as he knows, I'm a legit client, here for his spooky services."

"What did you tell him you needed?"

Lucas grinned. "I told him that my great uncle died before

I could ask him where he kept his cash. See, he didn't trust the banks, so he stashed it in a locker somewhere."

"That's quite a detailed make-believe story you've got going."

"I always wanted to find a buried treasure."

"Aha. So you're part soldier, part pirate."

Lucas chuckled and veered to the left. "This way."

"How do you know?" I asked, glancing behind me. Had I missed some giant *here's the creepy voodoo guy's apartment* sign?

"Google Maps, baby."

I rolled my eyes.

Annoying or not, it worked. A line of apartments stood to our left and the one on the end bore the gaudy gold numbers identifying is as 17A. "We good?" Lucas asked as we stopped just short of the tattered welcome mat.

I looked to my left and my right. Gwen and Sturgeon flanked Lucas. Flapjack was at my feet, Hayward at my shoulder. "We're good."

He knocked and I held my breath.

I don't know what I was expecting, but the man who answered the door would never have even made the list. We just stared at each other for the span of a couple of heartbeats, then I found my voice. "Franklin? But ... but how? You're supposed to be dead!"

The door slammed shut.

CHAPTER 22

Lucas looked from the door to me, confused. "Safe to say you two know each other?"

I didn't answer him. I was too busy pounding on the door as if I was part of a SWAT unit. "Open up, Franklin!"

"Scarlet! Who is he?" Gwen floated around until she was in my line of vision.

"Franklin Boules. He was a ghost from when I lived in Arizona. Every day he would come to my parents' house and beg me to make him a human again. He refused to take no for an answer even though I tried to get it through his thick skull that it wasn't possible. Over time, he got really nasty and I had no choice but to banish him."

I started pounding again. "Franklin, open this door right now!"

Lucas stepped between the door and me. "Scarlet, you have to stop. All this is going to do is bring the cops around. Okay?"

"Myra and Quinton are in there! That's *just* the kind of

thing he'd do to get back at me. He probably saw them leave my shop, assumed we were friends, and found some way to—to ghostnap them."

"I don't like this, Scar," Flapjack said. "How does he have a—a body?"

I glanced down at my feet. Flapjack sat close enough that if still living, I would have felt him against my leg. He was clearly shaken up. And if Flapjack was freaked out, then something was really wrong. "I don't know."

"Scoot over," Lucas said, shuffling me to the side. He retrieved something from his pocket and went to work on the lock.

"You can pick locks?"

He flashed a wicked grin. "Greene. Lucas Greene."

Less than a minute later, Lucas turned the knob and threw the door open. I raced ahead, but he pulled me back. "Wait!" Lucas growled. "We don't know what other tricks this guy has up his sleeves."

Begrudgingly, I let him go into the apartment first. My motley crew of the dead weren't as patient. Gwen surged past us, Sturgeon right at her heels. Even Hayward raced ahead. Flapjack was the only one who stayed close to me.

"Franklin! We know you're in here!" I called out as we fanned into the living room.

The inside was much like the exterior of the building: dated and ran-down.

Just off the living room were a dining nook and a galley kitchen. Past that was a small hallway. Lucas jerked his head, indicating for me to follow, and we crept through the kitchen and into the hall. One of the bedroom doors was ajar and when I pushed it open, I would have laughed if the situation hadn't been so dire.

It looked like the hokey psychic's tent at a traveling fair.

Black-out curtains hung from the windows, leaving glow-in-the-dark stickers and a lava lamp to provide the only light. Still, it was enough to see a crystal orb and what I assumed was a scrying mirror placed on a table draped in gaudy, royal-blue crushed velvet.

"Classy." I wrinkled my nose. I couldn't imagine anyone actually overlooking the appearance of the place long enough for a séance or palm reading. Or whatever the heck it was that Franklin was doing.

Lucas went to the accordion doors blocking a small closet and flung them open. It was stuffed with boxes and clothing. No sign of Franklin.

"Where is he?" I asked under my breath, turning in a slow circle.

"Scar, I think we should leave." Flapjack peered out into the hall. "I don't like the feel of this place."

"We aren't leaving until we know what's going on," I replied.

"I know," Lucas said, thinking I was talking to him.

Before I could explain, Sturgeon's voice called out from somewhere deeper in the apartment. "Down here!"

I pivoted back toward the door and pointed down the hall. "Sturgeon just yelled for us."

"Come on, Flapjack," I said as Lucas bounded back out of the room. My once-fuzzy companion muttered something under his breath and followed after him.

Sturgeon stood at a closed door, his silvery face drawn. "Brace yourself."

"What is it?" I asked.

Lucas yanked open the door, revealing a steep flight of stairs down to another level. No light, of course.

"Oh, good. A creepy basement. That's what we were missing," Flapjack quipped.

"What's down there, Sturgeon?"

He opened his mouth, ready to offer an explanation, when his eyes bulged. He clawed at his throat, like his air supply had been cut off, which, of course, was ridiculous. He didn't *need* air. But the frantic look in his eyes and jerking movements of his hands couldn't be ignored.

"Sturgeon! What's happening?" I reached out, forgetting that I couldn't touch him until my hand was almost on his arm. There was nothing I could do to help him.

He yanked one hand away from his throat long enough to gesture wildly at the door. "Go!" he wheezed. "Find. Gwen."

My heart slammed into my chest. "Lucas, go! Something's wrong! We have to find the others!"

Lucas pulled the Taser from his hip and barreled down the stairs. "We just want to talk," he called out into the darkness.

"Flapjack, go find Hayward!" I ordered, not waiting for his argument before descending after Lucas.

Another door blocked the way at the end of the stairs. Lucas reached for his side and produced a flashlight. Seconds later, a high-powered beam flooded the small space with light. "What is this? Some kind of panic room?"

My stomach curled into a tight knot. Something told me that whatever was on the other side was nothing like the silly props we'd found upstairs. The air was charged with something that made all the hairs on my arms stand up.

Lucas tried the doorknob. "It's locked."

"Can you kick it in? Pick it? Something! We have to hurry," I told him. Flapjack was no longer at my side. I hadn't seen Hayward or Gwen. And for all I knew, Sturgeon was still choking at the top of the stairs.

Lucas didn't answer me. In a calm manner that was equal parts comforting and infuriating, he went to work on the lock, just as he had the one on the front door. There were three locks total. The fact that whatever was behind it was so heavily guarded didn't do anything to assuage my fears. Every second ticked by at an agonizing crawl.

Finally, Lucas huffed and the last lock sprung. He jerked the metal door open and light poured into the small outer chamber from the room beyond. I wanted to shove him forward, to yell and spur him on faster, but was too terrified to speak.

"Lady Scarlet!"

My heart jumped. "Hayward!"

I spun around and found Flapjack and Hayward behind me. I'd never wanted to hug a ghost so badly in my life. "What's going on? What did you see?"

A loud crash sounded before they could answer.

"Scarlet! Look out!"

Lucas ducked back into the small chamber and a split second later, glass shattered. "He's throwing dishes or jars or something!"

"Have either of you seen Gwen?" I asked Hayward and Flapjack.

They both shook their heads.

"I think she's in trouble. Sturgeon too."

Hayward puffed out his chest, adjusted his top hat. "That will not stand!"

Without another word, he flew through the door.

"Go away!" a high-pitched voice squealed.

"That was Franklin!" I told Lucas. "Little worm. He's not going to get away with this."

"We don't even know what *this* is, Scarlet." Lucas flinched as another glass slammed into the wall and broke.

"Well, I'm not going to stand here and wait anymore. I'm going in and finding out!"

Lucas grabbed for me, but I swerved and zipped past him.

"Scarlet!" he hissed. "This guy is obviously unbalanced. And possibly undead. Is it really wise to—"

"Franklin, what are you—" I stopped short, as I realized what I was looking at.

The large room was set up like a laboratory, but instead of bright, fluorescent lights, the space was illuminated with sacs of light that glowed in jewel tones, blue, purple, green. Each pool of light trapped a ghost inside, like some sort of pod.

The air in my lungs evaporated as my eyes found familiar faces; Myra, Quinton, Ruthie, and ... Gwen.

"Oh my gosh. What is this?" I covered my mouth to contain a sob.

Gwen pounded on the walls of her container, screaming, though I couldn't hear a word.

"Lady Scarlet!"

My gaze pinged toward Hayward's voice, and a roar broke free. "No!"

Hayward was frozen in place, light pooling at his ankles, rising quickly. Soon, he would be trapped too. Just like the others.

"You shouldn't have come here, Scarlet."

The cold voice belonged to the man in the center of the room.

"Franklin." I narrowed my eyes at him and mustered every ounce of bravado I could find. "I don't know what the hell happened to you, but you can be damn sure that I'm not leaving until all of these ghosts are freed."

He responded by hurling a glass bottle at my head. I sidestepped it and bumped into Lucas, who was once again at my side. He raised his Taser. I glanced at him, wondering exactly how much of the horrific scene he could even see. Would he see the ghosts trapped? I doubted it. But whatever he saw, it was clear from the set of his jaw, he knew it was deadly serious.

Franklin laughed as he considered Lucas's weapon. "If you hurt me, you'll never get your little friends loose. So, I suggest you listen up."

My stomach rolled as my eyes zoomed to Myra. She'd been missing the longest. She was despondent, her eyes unfocused pinpoints. What was he doing to her? To all of them?

"I figured you'd eventually put the pieces together and find out what was happening. So I created a contingency plan."

I glared at him. "I'm not here to make a deal. You're going to let them go, and you're not leaving here a free ... whatever you are."

Lucas stepped forward.

Franklin laughed and I realized how flimsy my threat must have sounded. It was clear that he was playing in a *whole* different league than me. "Oh, Scarlet. Your threats don't mean much. Not anymore. You can't banish me away from you this time. I have my body again. And as long as I have a steady supply of ghosts, I'll keep it. Forever."

A chill ran down my spine. "You're *feeding* off of other ghosts?"

Across the room, Hayward made a gurgling, choking sound. The light was almost to his chin. "Hayward!"

"Don't worry about me, Lady Scarlet. Save the—"

The light sac sealed around him and the rest of his words were muted. Panic surged through me so hard I nearly threw up. I screamed and hurled myself toward Franklin. "Let him go you leech!"

"Scarlet!" Lucas and Flapjack yelled in unison.

I reached Franklin before they could reel me back. My

hands wrapped around his throat and a sick glee took hold as fear entered his beady eyes.

"Scarlet! If you hurt him, we won't get them back!" Flapjack cried out.

"Tell me how to let them free!" I demanded, squeezing tighter as Franklin began to flail.

Lucas pried me off of him and pushed me back. "Scarlet, stop it! You're going to kill him!"

"He's not even alive!" I argued, my fingers itching to claw at the squirming monster again.

Lucas ignored me as he fought with Franklin, managing to twist him around and pin him face-first against the wall, his arms at odd angles behind his back. "Tell us what she wants, or I can promise this is going to get a lot more uncomfortable," he growled down into Franklin's ear.

"The orbs! It's the orbs!" Sturgeon shouted.

I whipped around and saw him fly into the room, frantically pointing at Hayward and I realized what he was talking about. There, in front of Hayward's metaphysical cage was a small stone. I hadn't noticed it before, but now it was obvious, glowing and pulsing a lava red.

"That's how he's caging them?" I said, noticing an orb in front of each trapped ghost.

Sturgeon nodded as his brow furrowed in concentration. He levitated the orb in front of Hayward and with a jerk of his head, sent it soaring into the wall. It shattered into hundreds of pieces and the light pinning Hayward fizzled and then vanished.

"Nice work!" I hurried to Myra and smashed her orb at my feet. The trap relented but she didn't move. "Get her out of here, Sturgeon!"

Franklin wailed. "No! Stop it!"

Ignoring his cries, I continued down the line, destroying the orbs as Lucas held him against the wall. One by one, they shattered and the bubbles faded, freeing another ghost.

"Get out of here! Run as far away as you can!" I screeched at them.

Sturgeon reached for Myra and then for Ruthie once she was free. He took them each by the wrist and they fled. Quinton bolted as soon as I freed him, Gwen moments later. She called out for Quinton but he was already gone. Her face crumpled and she went to stand with Hayward who was speaking with Flapjack. I couldn't hear what they were saying; their voices were drowned out by relieved ghosts calling their thanks, orbs smashing against the wall, and Franklin's hysterical pleas for us to stop.

"A real special kind of sicko, huh? Torturing the dead?" Lucas called out above the noise, once the last orb was broken. He released his hold on him and Franklin crab-walked to the nearest wall, flattening himself against it. His face was drained of all color as his chest heaved.

I turned to Hayward and Flapjack. "You two, search the rest of the house. Make sure we aren't leaving anyone behind."

"Yes, my lady!"

"What he said."

They left and I lunged at Franklin. "How dare you!"

He panted, each breath ragged. "It was the only way, Scarlet! No one else could help me. Then, I met a voodoo priest. He helped me."

"Why here in Beechwood Harbor? Just to get back at me?"

His face went purple. Somehow, he was running out of air, even as his chest continued to rise and fall. "You banished me! Do you know what that's like for a ghost?"

I barked out a sharp, hysterical laugh. "You can't be serious! Do you not see what you were doing to these ghosts? How many have you destroyed?"

"They were ghosts no one wanted around! I put out an ad for my services. When I find someone, like Dr. Barnes, who wants a ghost gone, I take them with me. They stay here. They don't feel pain!"

"That's disgusting!" I clenched my fists, eager to get another crack at him. "And my friends were not *unwanted*."

He looked down at his feet. "When I saw that you were helping them, I got angry. You refused to help me, but there you were, holding meetings, helping any ghost who asked. Why not me?"

I threw my hands up. "Because all you wanted was your old life back! You didn't want to move on or learn how to be a ghost! When I told you that I couldn't help, I meant it. You were asking for the impossible. Or, at least, what I *thought* was impossible. You obviously found a loophole, but I would have never helped you with something like this. It's —it's sick!"

"I—" his words choked off. No longer powered by his ghost-fueled generators, Franklin slowly faded. Turning from a corporeal body to the ghost version I was familiar with in a matter of seconds. The clothes and spectacles he'd been wearing as a human slid to the floor and pooled at his once-again silvery legs that were clothed in the slacks and cardigan sweater I remembered.

"This time, I'm not taking any chances," I said, reaching for an orb that sat on his desk. It wasn't lit up red like the others. I figured it was waiting to be used and stepped forward, waving it in his face.

"No!" he screamed. "Anything but that!"

"Then leave this town," I hissed, inches from his face. "Never come back. And if I catch wind of any more of these shenanigans, I'll personally put you in one of these orbs and throw you into the ocean!"

"Ye—yes, Scarlet. I—I promise."

He vanished with a loud *pop*, leaving me and Lucas gaping at one another.

"You believe him?" he asked after a moment.

"I don't know. But it gives me some time to learn how this thing works," I replied, slipping the orb into my pocket.

A lopsided grin tugged at Lucas's lips. "You were bluffing?"

"That's what Bond would do, right?"

CHAPTER 23

News of Drea's arrest reached us a couple of weeks later, courtesy of Gwen, who had resumed her regular fly-by visits a few times a week. I knew it would take some time to get back to the way it used to be between us but we were working on it. Everyone, in fact, was a little shaken following the confrontation at Franklin's house of ghosty horrors. I'd visited the ghosts as my overbooked schedule allowed, and there didn't seem to be any permanent effects. Myra regained her ability to speak and move, though from Gwen's reports, she wasn't doing much of either.

Kimberly listened to the ghosts accounts and I got the sense that she was sorry she'd missed out on all the excitement. In the weeks since her death, she'd come quite a way from the shallow, self-absorbed woman I'd met several months before. She was barely recognizable as the snob who'd barely uttered a hello before burying me in a dumpster full of bridal magazines and fabric swatches. We still weren't destined to be BFFs, but my tolerance level for her had increased. I didn't feel the urge to heave a beleaguered sigh every time she came floating into the room.

So, when she arrived at the shop on the day I'd heard of her sister's arrest, I was relieved when she informed me that she'd already heard the news and that she was okay with it. The family lawyer had brokered a deal with the DA and Drea would serve a few years in prison and then be required to give back via community service. Despite Kimberly's original fire-and-brimstone approach to her unintentional murder, she'd softened since finding out it had been at her sister's hand.

Still, I suspected she wasn't likely to visit her anytime soon.

"What's next then? Now that this is all sorted out?" I asked her, while Lizzie was busy taking inventory in the cooler.

She sighed. "I don't know. I thought I'd be ready to cross over by now, but I'm starting to think that it might be nice to hang around a little while longer."

"Just as long as you don't mean *here* here," Flapjack chimed in.

Kimberly shot him a glare. "Oh, shut up. You'll miss me once I'm gone."

"Where are you going to go?"

She fluffed her hair. "I might go down to California and see what it's like being a beach bunny. At least there will be some good man candy to ogle."

I laughed. "Sounds like a plan."

"The start of one at least." She dropped her eyes to her hands. "Before I left, I wanted to let you know that I really do appreciate everything you did for me."

"And here I thought that thank you wasn't in her vocabulary," Flapjack said.

"Shh! Scat, cat!" I said, flapping a hand at him.

Kimberly met my eyes and smiled. "I mean it, Scarlet. Thank you."

Tears blurred my vision and I quickly blinked them away. "You're welcome, Kimberly. I'll be around if you ever need anything."

Flapjack scoffed.

Kimberly and I laughed and then she gave a slight wave and floated back toward the front doors.

"See, Flapjack, it always comes around full circle."

He circled in the dapples of sunlight in front of the window and curled up. "If you say so."

~

Toward the end of his stay in Beechwood Harbor, Lucas was called back to L.A. to participate in the final stages of the planning meetings. Logistical boot camp, he'd called it, as his main job would be getting his new underlings in line. He'd stayed loyal to the show for several years, but the lower-level positions tended to roll over each season. Onto greener pastures ... or, greener basements?

The timing worked in my favor because I had a final push of weddings to get through. Even though Kimberly's wedding hadn't ended up being the first, several events were held at the Lilac B&B over the following months, all of which required copious amounts of flowers. This was good for my bank account but murder on my feet and lower back. And don't get me started on the pesky little lines under my eyes caused by sleep deprivation.

I also had a suspicion that I would go full-blown Hulk if I had to make one more pew bow. Luckily, it turned out that Lizzie's slippery little fingers were quite adept when working with ribbons and I'd been able to farm out most of the final weddings of the season to her. As far as I was concerned, she earned a place on my staff for that trait alone.

"Another one in the books," I told Lizzie on the last

GHOSTS GONE WILD

Saturday in August. She'd just returned from dropping off an arrangement at Siren's Song for their annual end-of-summer bash, which was sort of the town's final act for the year. Holly told me it was more of an excuse to close early and bust out some adult beverages to celebrate reclaiming the town from the tourists until the next season.

Lizzie put the van's keyring in its spot in the register drawer. "Got any plans for the weekend?"

I shrugged. "Not really. Looks like I'll be spending it alone."

The weekly ghost meetings had petered out since Gwen wasn't around to organize them anymore. Flapjack and Hayward still came and went as they pleased, but seemed to be spending more time out of the shop. It was a good thing for them, but I couldn't help feeling a little lonely, especially with Lucas out of town. But I supposed that was going to be my new normal. Lucas only had a week left of vacation before he'd be back to traveling with the show, and I'd be left behind, running my shop and resisting the urge to abandon my new business and run off on some grand adventure.

Lucas had given up the hard sell, but I knew the offer was still there, lingering just under the surface. All I had to do was say the word and he'd start cooking up a plan.

My parents—specifically my mother—would want to wring my neck. But that wasn't the part that bothered me. It was more the idea that I'd be squandering the inheritance money my grandmother had left me to get my shop open in the first place. If I gave up now, it would be a disservice to her memory.

"What about you?" I asked, considering Lizzie as she hesitated at the register, looking over the schedule for the following week. I couldn't help wondering why she wasn't scampering out the door, ready to get her weekend started.

After all, she wasn't even twenty-one. Didn't she have a horde of friends to go out with?

Lizzie smiled and shook her head when I asked. "No, at least, nothing big."

I folded my arms. "Can I ask you something?"

"Of course."

"Do you like working here?"

She looked up, startled. "Of course I do!"

"What would you say to coming on full-time?" I asked her.

That threw her even further off kilter. Her eyes went wide and her thin brows arched into peaks.

"I know that things will slow down now that summer is almost over, but with the Lilac B & B booked out, we'll have plenty of orders from them. I was just speaking with Mitchel and he assured me things will be steady. Then add in normal, local business and some canvassing of nearby towns, and it's a lot for one person."

Lizzie started nodding vigorously. "I'd love to! Gosh, I was worried for a minute there. I thought you were going to fire me!"

"Fire you?"

She tucked her chin. "I know I've cost the company—you —some money. What with the van repairs and the broken vases, coffee pot, and that water leak in the cooler …"

Leak was a mild way of putting the three inches of standing water that had flooded the walk-in after she'd left the neighboring utility sink running all night long the first week of her employment.

I flapped a hand. "Mistakes happen."

Granted, they seemed to happen to Lizzie more frequently than most.

"I want to expand my business, but also have some free time. I know I can trust you. You're a hard worker, you're honest with me, and our customers love you. So, if you're game, I'd love to bring you on full-time, starting in October."

Lizzie smiled and I knew I'd made the right choice. "Thank you, Scarlet! I would be thrilled."

"Great. I'll have some paperwork for the benefits ready on Tuesday. For now, get on out of here. Go enjoy yourself."

"Okay!" She bobbed her head, still grinning ear to ear, and hurried out the back door.

I chuckled to myself after she'd gone. "Wait till I tell Flapjack."

∼

When I emerged from the office a couple of hours later, I wasn't alone.

"Hello, Gwen," I said as my friend stood sentinel at the front window. "Are you waiting on someone?"

"No. I just couldn't think of anywhere else to go," she replied without turning around to look at me.

"Is everything okay?" I asked, going to the register to grab my keys. "You haven't been around here in a while."

She reached up and toyed absently with one of her dangling feather earrings. "I'm sure it will be. Quinton and I parted ways."

"I'm sorry, Gwen." I hated to feel like I was pulling teeth, but after the last few frosty weeks, I was ready to make peace and if a little prodding would get things started, I'd have to suck it up. "Do you want to talk about it?"

She finally turned toward me, wearing an expression that matched her somber tone. "I don't like not talking to you, Scarlet."

"I don't like it either."

A flicker of a smile crossed her lips. "That's good to hear."

I drew in a slow breath. "Listen, Gwen, I'm really sorry

about the way things went the past few weeks. With Myra and Quinton."

She waved a hand. "It's already forgotten, Scarlet. Besides, if anyone should be asking for forgiveness it's me. I should have trusted you."

"Don't give it a second thought. It was a *beyond* strange situation. I'm just glad we're all okay."

"Ditto."

"Come on," I said, beckoning for her to follow me. My stomach was reminding me that I hadn't had anything since the coffee and muffin when I'd sent Lizzie over to Siren's Song to get us breakfast—another perk of having a second pair of hands on staff. "I'm gonna grab a bite upstairs. Come tell me what's going on around town."

She grinned widely and rushed forward but then faltered, her gaze nervously drifting to the ceiling. "Um, is Hayward upstairs?"

"No. He and Flapjack have been going out a lot lately. I'm not entirely sure what they're up to. Truthfully, I don't know if I *want* to know. It's nice just having them out of my hair."

Gwen smiled and laughed softly. "I can only imagine."

"You know, eventually, you'll have to—"

She nodded. "I know."

"All right. I'll leave it alone, then." It wouldn't be easy, but as she'd just said, we needed to trust one another. Gwen would make things right, and I had no doubt that Hayward would warm back up to her in time.

She followed me upstairs, chattering away about everything from the latest updates on the McGuire divorce to the raging argument at city hall over what color to stain the benches and picnic tables at the local park. I listened to her enthused ramblings as I puttered around the kitchen, whipping up a grilled cheese sandwich and warming up a huge bowl of barley stew to accompany it.

While I ate, she floated through the apartment, inspecting things with a casual eye. I knew what she was doing—snooping for signs of Lucas.

"He's in L.A.," I finally told her as she made her second pass through the living room.

"What? Who? Oh, um, you mean Lucas."

Gwen was many things, but an actress wasn't one of them.

I laughed. "He'll be back in a few days."

She broke into a wide smile. "So, things are going well?"

I nodded and took a bite of my sandwich.

"New book?" Gwen asked.

I turned to see what she was referring to and nearly dropped the tea kettle. *The Magic Gardner*, the textbook—the *magic* textbook—Holly had given me several months ago had somehow ended up on the coffee table. My fingers trembled and I set my sandwich aside. "What—what is that doing there?"

Gwen looked at me, her brows furrowed. "What do you mean?"

"I mean, I didn't put it there. It's been on that shelf ever since Holly gave it to me."

"Oh dear." Gwen swooped closer but then quickly backtracked away from the book.

"No one else has been in here. At least not by themselves. I would have noticed if Lucas had taken some interest in it." I stepped into the living room and peered down at the book, halfway wondering if it was some kind of trick. Holly had been after me, in her own gentle prodding sort of way, since she gave it to me. It was her book and she was a witch ... maybe she'd made it move?

Was that even possible?

"Why did Holly give you the book?" Gwen asked.

"I don't know. Well, I mean, she said it was a textbook

from when she was in magic school. Academy, I think she called it. She thought maybe I would find it interesting."

Gwen's narrowed gaze went wide. "She thinks you're a witch!"

"No!" I hurried to the table, snatched up the book, and shoved it back into place on the shelf. "She said it's about plants and stuff. General studies, I'm sure."

"Um, Scarlet, those are runes on the spine. You see that, right?"

I sighed. "Okay, fine. Holly *might* have a tiny little suspicion that there is more to my ability than just the ghost stuff."

"Ooo."

I held up a hand. "Nope. Stop! We are not going to get all riled up about this. As of right now, it's nothing more than a hunch."

Gwen glided over toward me. "Well, what did Holly say you're supposed to do with the book?"

I shrugged. "Read it?"

"And have you?"

"No."

She frowned. "Why not?"

"Because…," I hesitated, alternating between trying to find a way to change the subject and actually coming up with an answer. So far, I hadn't been able to come to terms with my own feelings on the matter. All I knew was that if I cracked open the book, something would be revealed. Either there was more to my gift or there wasn't. Both of the possibilities scared me, for different reasons.

I'd wanted to know where my gift came from for as long as I could remember, but after so many years of searching, I'd grown used to the mystery. It was comforting to me in some weird way. Opening the book could rip that all away from me.

"I think you should try it," Gwen said, not waiting for me to form a full reply.

"Well that's not going to happen tonight, okay?"

Gwen sighed but didn't push farther. "All right. Well, in that case, I guess I'd better go figure out what Flapjack and Hayward are getting into. Goodness knows someone has to keep tabs on them."

"It does take a village."

Gwen laughed as she started for the door, only to stop short. One arm floated through the metal door, while the rest of her remained in my apartment. "I'm glad we're friends again."

"Gwen, we were never *not* friends," I replied. "But I know what you mean, and I'm glad too."

She smiled and then shimmied through the door.

The sudden silence in the apartment was overwhelming and I hurried to turn on the small stereo in the kitchen. I needed something to fill the void. Even with the distraction of the music and cooking one of only a few home-cooked meals since Lucas's arrival in town, my mind kept circling back to the book.

Finally, I surrendered. While the veggie lasagna finished baking, I stalked out to the bookshelf and removed the offending book. It was a large volume—several hundred pages filled the space between the covers. Each page was actually a thick piece of parchment that added weight and austerity to the tome.

After a moment, I dragged in a deep breath and took the book to the couch. I tucked my legs up underneath me and lifted the front cover. For a moment, I didn't feel a thing—except relief.

Then, the lights in the room flickered.

I told myself it was just a power surge but couldn't shake the spooky feeling.

"Where is that blabbermouth cat when you need him?" I muttered, reaching across the couch to snag the throw blanket off the opposite arm. "The Magic Gardner, A Collection of Basic spells, perfect for the little witch or wizard in your life." I frowned and peeked at the front cover. "Is this thing for real?"

A nagging voice told me to keep going. To give it a chance. I flipped the page, carefully, and saw that someone had scrawled a dedication in the front section:

To Holly,

Follow your heart. ***It will never lead you astray.***

Love,

Aunt Bethany

"Hmm." I frowned at the words, but a small boost of courage took root and I found the table of contents. As Holly had promised, the beginning section of the book was general information. Study guides and encyclopedia-like entries that introduced me to a whole new botanical world. Some of the florals and foliage were recognizable, familiar even, but then as I continued to flip through the book, I encountered drawings and lifelike photos of things I'd never seen before. Heartsong, Fairy Thistle, Graveyard Ivy. I drank in each page, taking my time to read each word, but then rushing to flip to the next one just as soon as I finished.

When the oven timer went off, I nearly leapt out of my skin. I threw the blanket off my lap and launched halfway across the living room, leaving the book behind as I went into the kitchen to check on my dinner.

Lasagna in hand, I returned and continued reading. The second half was basic spells. Specifically, gardening spells, from the looks of it. I'd mentioned to Holly that sometimes, when I was working with flowers and creating arrangements in my studio, it seemed like the plants had some intuitive bent, capturing what was in my head and almost moving a fraction of a second faster than my fingers.

I'd often wondered if it were actually the flowers leading the way and my fingers following, rather than the other way around.

The first page listed an incantation to spur growth. The diagrams that followed showed what looked like the top of a carrot stem growing in size following the text of the spell.

"Here goes ... everything," I said, exhaling as I got up from the couch. I abandoned my dinner and went to the kitchen where I had an assortment of small potted plants in the window. I grabbed one, noticing my fingers had started to shake, and took it out to the table. I knelt down and placed the potted plant on one side. I practiced the gesture with my fingers a couple of times, then whispered the words as best as I could.

Nothing happened.

Reciting the words, louder the second time, I tried once again. The room fell silent as I finished and I stared at the small plant for so long that my eyes started to burn. But still, nothing changed.

A surprising sense of defeat and disappointment swept over me. I rocked back onto my heels and braced my back against the couch.

"Guess that answers that question," I finally said in a small voice.

I snapped the book shut and took it over to the small table where I kept my keyring and spare change. I set it down, promising myself I'd take it back to Holly the next day. She'd probably be disappointed too, but at least we knew the truth.

CHAPTER 24

"What's going on?" I asked, glancing at the empty suitcase on the bed.

"Just a little something I picked up for you," Lucas replied, pocketing his hands. "I noticed the one in the hall closet is a little worse for the wear. Figured you could use an upgrade."

I went to the luggage and ran my finger along the stitching at the sides. It was top quality. That much was obvious with a single swipe. "This must have cost a small fortune," I said, mostly to myself.

"Don't worry about it."

"Well, uh, thank you. It's beautiful. Hopefully I'll get to use it sometime."

Lucas grinned. "I was hoping you'd say that."

I turned around. "What are you up to?"

"I spoke with your assistant and she's agreed to watch the shop for you for a few days."

My heart lurched. "Lizzie?" I asked, unable to keep a slight cringe out of my voice.

Lucas didn't seem to notice. "Yeah. As much time as I've spent on the West Coast, I've never been able to do a road trip down the 101. I thought we'd see about fixing that. We'll start here and head south, stopping in whatever little beach town catches our eye. See how far we get in five days and then spend another three or four coming back."

"Lucas, I don't think I can leave right now."

He crossed his arms. "Scarlet, come on. You've been working fifty hours a week since I got into town and that's not even counting the spooky extracurriculars. You need a break."

"He's right, you know," Flapjack chimed in.

"Oh, hush," I snapped at the cat.

Lucas flashed a triumphant smile. "See?" He hadn't heard Flapjack, but he'd been around enough over the past weeks to get to know his personality after my frequent translating.

I sighed, clearly outnumbered and too tired to argue further. "Lizzie really thinks she can handle it?" I asked, knowing that the girl would likely agree to anything if she thought it would help prove her worth and secure her job after her frequent mistakes in the beginning of her employment. She'd gotten better, but I was still shaky about the idea of leaving her the entire store in her hands.

Still, I did need to get away. Why not?

"Whoa! Looks like it might be time to get this guy a new home."

I followed Lucas's voice into the kitchen and squealed when I realized what he was talking about.

There in the kitchen window sat the small potted plant I'd tried to enchant the night before.

Only, instead of occupying a three-inch terra-cotta pot, the leaves had tripled in size and were spilling down the sides and hanging off the shelf, dangling over the kitchen sink.

"You been feeding this thing plant steroids?" Lucas teased.

I tried to smile, but couldn't do anything but stare. I guess *now* the question was answered.

~

"I can't believe summer is almost over."

Lucas pulled his gaze away from the sunset and smiled at me from his place across the small bistro table. We were having our final dinner together al fresco at a quaint waterfront eatery that overlooked the mouth of the harbor where it fed into the sea. "There are still a few weeks left," he said.

"Well, not for you."

He reached out and took my hand. "It's not going to be easy to say goodbye to this place, to you."

My eyes burned as I swallowed hard to drive down the lump in my throat. "Nine months is a long time," I said quietly. "Are we being naive here?"

Lucas squeezed my fingers. "Don't think about that right now."

I knew he was right. Dwelling on it all night wouldn't change anything and would sap away the joy left in the time remaining to us. His plane left the following afternoon and it would be best to simply enjoy each other. But it was hard when the thought of saying goodbye brought tears to my eyes. Somehow, against all odds, Lucas had found a way into my heart and even though I still had no idea where it was all headed, it was getting harder to imagine life without him around.

But for now, our time together was nearing an end. Whether we wanted to or not, we were heading into uncharted waters.

Lucas ordered us two more glasses of wine and we settled in to watch the last lingering minutes of the sunset.

"Should we toast to something?" I asked when the server returned with our wine.

Lucas lifted his glass and held it toward mine. "Safe to say that we're making this thing official?"

"This *thing*?" I repeated, grinning up at him. "Now *that's* romantic."

"What can I say? I'm a real smooth talker."

"I've noticed." I fidgeted with the stem of my glass.

Lucas's eyes darkened. "Scarlet, you know where I stand."

I nodded. "I do."

He paused, waiting for me to fill in the space, but my tongue tangled together and knotted up on the words I wanted to say. After a moment, he cleared his throat. "Maybe we should just toast to the summer?"

"Lucas, I— "

"Scarlet, I'm not going to rush you or ask for something you don't want to give to me."

"No, no!" I waved a hand. "That's not what this is. I'm just …" I drew in a shaky breath. "I'm just terrible at this stuff."

I looked past his shoulder, finding a rare moment where I actually *wished* there was a ghost hovering over us. At least maybe they could have fed me lines.

"Lucas, I know this is going to be tough. Time apart is rough on even the most established relationships. We're probably a little crazy, but hey, that's where I live. Crazyville, USA."

He laughed. "Sounds fun."

"I'll send you a postcard sometime."

"Scarlet," he said, stroking his thumb over my knuckles. "The best thing about living lives like ours is that we've learned to be really flexible. I'm not looking for ordinary and I know you aren't either. Sure, it might get messy and complicated, but I'm thinking we're both already good at handling the hard stuff. You don't travel the entire world and not know how to improvise."

"That's true."

"I get breaks every six weeks in between shoots. I can come here or you can fly to me. We'll figure it out."

I smiled. "You're sure?"

"Absolutely." He lifted his glass a second time. "Cheers to that?"

I smiled as relief flooded my stomach, driving out the pit of fear that had been camping out there for way too long. After Kimberly and Ruth were sorted out, Lucas and I found that the earlier hiccups in our relationship started to fade to the background, and despite the more-than-occasional ghostly interruptions, we ended up having a summer for the record books.

The past six weeks with Lucas had been something out of a fairy tale—or, at the very least, a really good rom-com. Late night conversations on the sand surrounded by a blanket of stars, fancy dinners at some of the area's finest restaurants, and casual nights in with a pizza and Netflix. The road trip down the Washington coast into Oregon went off without a hitch, filled with good food, campfires on the beach, and the best part—instead of coming home to a pile of cinders and some majorly pissed off ghosts, I found that Lizzie had kept the shop up and running without a hitch.

My glass met his with a tiny *clank*. "Cheers to figuring it out."

We each took a sip, smiling at each other over the rims of our respective glasses. When Lucas set his glass aside, he shifted in his seat and then reached into the interior of his casual suit jacket. "In that case, there is actually something I wanted to ask you."

My heart surged into my throat and for one panic-attack-inducing moment, I thought he was reaching into the pocket of his jacket for a ring box. Instead, he retrieved a white envelope. With a smile, he handed it to me and sat back while I opened it.

"What is this?" I asked, even as I sliced one fingernail under the flap.

"The first reno of the season is of an old hotel down in NOLA."

I dumped out the contents of the envelope and found a printed boarding pass for a flight to New Orleans. The dates were three weeks out with a week in between the departure and return flight.

"I want you to come visit me on set. See what kind of trouble we could get ourselves into."

I raised an eyebrow. "In New Orleans? AKA the ghost capital of the world?"

Lucas chuckled. "Well, I did consider the possibility that the hotel the Carter's have purchased might have an infestation and that it would be a good idea to have all hands on deck. Just in case."

"Just in case?"

He laughed. "Come on. What do you say? We can have beignets and coffee and listen to some jazz. Get a tarot card reading?" He waggled his eyebrows.

I laughed. "What, did you read a tourist brochure before coming to dinner? There's more to NOLA than pastries and voodoo."

"You'll have to show me," he said. "It'll be my first visit, oddly enough."

"I see." Visions of walking the French Quarter, drinking in the architecture and laughing together about some shared joke from the night before floated in my head.

If nothing else, a week and a half away from the ghosts would be nice …

"All expenses paid," Lucas added, sweetening the pot.

"Okay," I replied, with a nod. "You've got a date."

After all, what better place that New Orleans to tell your boyfriend that you might have *more* magic powers.

AUTHOR'S NOTE

Thank you so much for reading Ghosts Gone Wild! I hope you enjoyed your return to Scarlet's world and, of course, to Beechwood Harbor. I really enjoy writing about Scarlet and her ghost pals. Sometimes I imagine her as a ventriloquist who has lost control of the puppets—it's all chatter, all the time! In the next book, When Good Ghosts Get the Blues, we will be hitting the road and heading to New Orleans for an extra magical story with some voodoo and a few new friends!

Grab your copy of When Good Ghosts Get the Blues. I promise you won't want to miss it!

Until next time,

Danielle Garrett
www.DanielleGarrettBooks.com

ACKNOWLEDGMENTS

First of all, I would like to thank my parents, who fed my love of reading from an early age. My sister, for supporting my desire to tell stories since I started "over complicating" our Barbie doll's lives.

For my handsome husband, you know how much I love you. I appreciate your daily support (and for listening to all of my writerly rants and keeping my caffeinated at all times).

Thank you to Theresa, my fabulous editor for all of your tips and kind words. And Keri, for the killer covers.

Writing can be a solitary passion, but with all of you beside me, it's never lonely.

Thank you.

ABOUT DANIELLE GARRETT

From a young age, Danielle Garrett was obsessed with fantastic places and the stories set within them. As a lifelong bookworm, she's gone on hundreds of adventures through the eyes of wizards, princesses, elves, and some rather wonderful everyday people as well.

Danielle now lives in Oregon and while she travels as often as possible, she wouldn't want to call anywhere else home. She shares her life with her husband and their house full of animals, and when not writing, spends her time being a house servant for three extremely spoiled cats and one outnumbered puppy.

For more about Danielle and her work, please visit her at:
www.daniellegarrettbooks.com
www.facebook.com/daniellegarrettbooks